"But

"That's nice. But you don't have to tell me all this," she whispered.

"I want to."

Marissa felt herself grow wondrously lost in the liquid-brown eyes that now shimmered like dark, exotic pools of moonlit-laced water. She moved her head back the scant distance it took for it to touch the wall.

"Why?" Her word was a mere puff of air.

"Because I don't want the past to stand between us." He lowered his head and kissed her tenderly, taking her breath away. "Because I want you to know what you're getting into," he murmured when he raised his head. "But most of all because I think I'm falling in love with you."

She gasped and jerked backward, her shoulders hitting the wall.

"Marissa?" His voice came out hoarse.

"I don't know what to say," she whispered.

"Then don't say anything. Just please, whatever you do, don't tell me there's no hope for us either."

This time when he kissed her, Marissa kissed him back. For mindless seconds she enjoyed nothing but Antonio's lips on hers, the security of his strong arms around her. She broke away and stared, shocked by her lack of sound judgment. What was she doing?

"I have to go," she blurted.

PAMELA GRIFFIN lives in Texas and divides her time among family, church activities, and writing. She fully gave her life to the Lord in 1988 after a rebellious young adulthood and owes the fact that she's still alive today to an all-loving and forgiving God and a mother who prayed that her wayward daughter would come "home." Pamela's main goal in writing Christian romance is to encourage others through entertaining stories that also heal the wounded spirit.

Please visit Pamela at:
http://members.cowtown.net/PamelaGriffin/

Books by Pamela Griffin

HEARTSONG PRESENTS

Don't miss out on any of our super romances. Write to us at the following address for information on our newest releases and club information.

Heartsong Presents Readers' Service
PO Box 721
Uhrichsville, OH 44683

Or visit www.heartsongpresents.com

A Single Rose

Pamela Griffin

Heartsong Presents

Bouquets of thanks to my critique partners and other writer friends for going above and beyond the call of duty in helping me. Also a heartfelt thank-you to Mary, for taking time from her duties in her florist shop to answer my many job-related questions. And a special thank-you to my two precious gems, Brandon and Joshua, who are the best sons a mom can have and who gave me a great line for this story when I needed it. As always, this is dedicated to my Lord Jesus, who freely gave His unconditional love to a thief who didn't know Him and reformed her into a giver who would do anything for Him.

A note from the Author:
I love to hear from my readers! You may correspond with me by writing:

> **Pamela Griffin**
> **Author Relations**
> **PO Box 719**
> **Uhrichsville, OH 44683**

ISBN 1-59310-114-7

A SINGLE ROSE

Our mission is to publish and distribute inspirational products offering exceptional value and biblical encouragement to the masses.

All Scripture quotations are taken from the King James Version of the Bible.

All of the characters and events in this book are fictitious. Any resemblance to actual persons, living or dead, or to actual events is purely coincidental.

PRINTED IN THE U.S.A.

one

"And in this corner, weighing in at a slight one hundred and thirty pounds, give or take a pound, and standing at the incredible height of five foot five inches—when she's standing—is Wadleyville's own professional dreamer and champion of the wild imagination—Marissa Hughes!"

Marissa shifted her focus from the smiling bridal couple on the wall calendar to her friend, who'd just waltzed into her office. "You know, Judy," she said in measured tones, "your husband's infatuation with boxing sounds as if it's starting to have an alarming effect on you."

Judy looked horrified. "Take that back, or I might not let you have this."

Curious, Marissa craned her neck, keeping her attention on the white paper parcel Judy held away from her. "That depends. What is it?"

Judy's round face broke into smiles. She opened the bag and held it under Marissa's nose. "Try one. It's a new recipe we're using. My own invention," she added proudly.

Marissa withdrew one of the soft powdered-sugar triangles and bit into it. Judy's pastries never failed to please. "Mmm. It reminds me of a Mexican wedding cookie, though it has a more distinct lemony flavor. And pineapple. And nuts! I love nuts." Marissa took another bite. "Our clients will find these irresistible."

"They're not just any nuts. They're macadamia nuts—the best there are And these are all for you." She set the bag on Marissa's desk. "Now I just need to come up with a name for them."

"You spoil me," Marissa said. She grabbed another cookie and polished it off. "It's great having a friend who owns a bakery next door and uses me as the official taste-tester. What's even better, I haven't been poisoned yet." Marissa cracked a smile but saw that her friend's attention had wavered from the subject of sweets.

Judy picked up the video Marissa had rented that morning. "Another *Thin Man* movie?" she asked in a level voice, her eyebrows lifted.

"Sherlock and I like watching old mystery movies," Marissa defended herself, shrugging. "You know that."

"Don't waste your breath, old friend. You can't convince me that at the age of twenty-five you'd rather stay home with your cat on a Saturday night and watch some detective flick from the '30s than go skating and to dinner with the singles."

Marissa snatched the video from Judy, who was tapping it against her palm. She secured it in her desk drawer before responding. "Wanna bet?"

"Grant won't be there. He's moved, remember?"

"This isn't about Grant," Marissa said, not wanting to discuss her ex-fiancé. "I just don't fit in. I don't understand the Internet or computers or the latest music. None of it appeals. DVD and CD are just groups of letters to me, which makes me rotten at trying to take part in many conversations." Marissa grinned. "I was born way after my time."

"You are anything but rotten at conversations." Judy shook her head. "You know what I think the real trouble is? All these weddings you've done lately have made you dream of your own wedding, and you're getting melancholy. You're ripe for love, Honey."

Marissa wrinkled her nose. "You make me sound like some strange sort of fruit. Anyway, the last thing I want to do after my experience with Grant is dwell on the subject of love."

Their conversation halted as Linda came from the florist section of the shop into Marissa's office. "May I have my break now? It's slow out there."

Marissa eyed the dark-haired seventeen year old, who had a passion for platform shoes and chewing gum—constantly clomping around in one and clacking the other. "All right," Marissa said, looking at her gold wristwatch bracelet. "I'll cover for you."

Once the teenager slipped on her jacket and exited the shop's front door, Judy crossed her arms. "Does she ever work? Every time I come in here she's on a break or going on one."

Marissa chuckled. "Linda's okay. Her talent for flower arrangements is really remarkable." She popped another cookie into her mouth.

The bell above the outside door to the florist shop jingled again. "Oops." Marissa stood and brushed off any white confectioner's sugar from her navy skirt and gray sweater. She spotted some sprinkled on her long blond hair, swept it away, then whisked her hands together. "I'm being summoned."

Judy was flipping through the latest bridal magazine sitting atop the huge stack on the desk. "Uh-huh."

Leaving her office, Marissa turned to the right and entered the small florist area. The fragrant aroma of flowers and plants mingled with the earthy, appealing odor of new sawdust and potted soil. She smiled and drew in a deep breath but forgot to exhale when her customer—a handsome brown-eyed stranger with wavy dark hair that hit just below his collar—entered her line of vision. He moved up to the counter, his stride fluid. A pair of black denim jeans and a navy blue sweatshirt clad a body that could pass any grueling physical, Marissa was sure. Lithe, strong, but not a wrestle-mania type of muscle man either.

"Hello. Can you help me?" His soft words rivaled the warmth in his coffee-rich eyes.

Feeling the sudden need to expel her oxygen, Marissa exhaled a soft wheezing cough. "Excuse me," she said, covering her mouth with one hand. She recovered and straightened, irritated with herself. She was acting as giddy as Linda did when one of the boys from the local high school sauntered through the door.

Marissa affected a businesslike smile. "Now how can I be of service to you this morning, Sir?"

"Please," he demurred. "Call me Antonio. I recently moved to your town. So you see we are practically neighbors." His gaze dropped to her mouth, and his beautifully shaped lips flickered at the corners, as though holding back a smile. "And you are—?" he asked, his gaze again meeting hers.

"I am—" She thought desperately. *Oh, no! What is my name?* "I'm Marissa Hughes," she said quickly. "I own this shop."

"Marissa." Her name coming from his lips was as smooth as the creamiest fondue. "Well, Marissa, I am in need of a fresh and fragrant yellow rose. One that has not yet fully bloomed." He delivered the lines as perfectly as a Latin actor might. How could he make a request for a flower sound so appealing?

"Of course," she managed. "I'll be right back."

Instead of pointing out the direction for him to go, as she would have for any other customer, Marissa moved from behind the counter toward the rear of the shop, needing temporary escape. Still, she wasn't surprised to hear his soft footfalls on the tile behind her.

Briefly she closed her eyes and tried to gather her wits. *Breathe, silly girl. He's just a man. You run across them every day.*

At the glass doors of the flower cooler, she turned and lifted her hand as a game show model might do. "Here they are," she said needlessly. Realizing she was making an absolute idiot of herself and seeing that he hadn't moved to open the door, she went toward it and grabbed the handle. Her gaze landed on her reflection in the glass, and she froze in horror.

A white powdered mustache winged up from the corners of her mouth.

Oh, no. She barely withheld the groan. Debating whether to shut the door, make a flimsy excuse and escape to the back office to wipe it off or just pretend it wasn't there, Marissa stood motionless for a few seconds. She lifted her hand and pretended to cough into it, at the same time slowly moving her fingers and thumb down, trying to wipe the white streaks away. A second glance at her reflection revealed that she'd only smeared them. Now two white splotches covered each side of her chin, and she had the beginnings of a powdered-sugar beard.

Gathering what few shreds of her dignity remained, she turned, hoping her polite smile wasn't as shaky as it felt. "I have three arrangements available."

To her astonishment Antonio reached into his back pocket and pulled out a blue bandana. He held it out to her, his expression one of amused sympathy. Heat flamed her face, and she felt as tongue-tied as the little girl who'd flubbed her school's chances for the district spelling bee by freezing up on stage. Only she'd been ten then, not an adult.

She accepted the cloth. "Thanks," she muttered.

He nodded. Seeming to recognize her need to regroup, he turned away to study several silk-flower baskets along the wall's two shelves. Quickly she dabbed her mouth with his warm kerchief. It bore the faint smell of car grease and musky cologne—a strange yet not unpleasant combination. Suddenly concerned that black streaks now replaced the white powder, Marissa whipped her gaze to her reflection, relieved to see that her fear was unfounded.

She folded the square of blue, grateful she wasn't wearing any lipstick to make matters worse, then handed the bandana to Antonio. Her gaze lifted to his steady warm stare then fluttered away. She retraced her steps to the cooler and pulled it open. The rubber lining made its customary sticking sound, and frigid air escaped. She studied the shelves of fresh flower arrangements Linda had made.

"Okay—so which one would you like?" she asked, managing to sound like her professional self again. "This is nice."

"Actually I'd prefer only one rose. Not several."

"Oh?" Marissa's brows lifted. "Well, all right. I don't usually keep single yellow roses on hand—only red ones and pink ones—there isn't a lot of call here for yellow roses. So I suppose I can take the other two roses out of this vase and give you the one. . .is the baby's breath okay to leave in, or do you want that removed as well? And the green frond behind it?"

To her shock he plucked one single yellow rose from the narrow glass vase she held. "I'll just take this."

"No vase?"

He smiled. "I don't need one."

"Oh." Marissa mentally cringed at her sudden astonishing lack of vocabulary. "I'll go wrap this up for you then."

"Thanks. I'd appreciate that."

She moved to the back room they used as a workroom, wrapped the rose in a half sheet of cellophane then tied it with a yellow satin ribbon. Returning to the counter, she rang up his purchase. Giving her a twenty-dollar bill, his fingers brushed her hand, and she almost dropped the money.

Her gaze briefly met his before flying to the open cash drawer. With lightning speed she dipped into separate compartments of coins and bills and pulled out what she hoped was the correct amount. She plunked the money into his outstretched palm, not bothering to count out his change. Her hands were too shaky for that, and she knew they'd wind up chasing coins all over the floor if she tried.

"Thank you, Marissa," Antonio said with another melting smile. "I'll be seeing you again soon."

Marissa gripped the edge of the counter and watched him go. Part of her dreaded the thought of another meeting with Antonio. The other part of her—the part that should be locked away—embraced it.

"Well!" Judy exclaimed softly. Marissa spun around to face her friend. The woman's plump cheeks were bunched in a smile as she watched Antonio's departing form through the front plate-glass window then looked back at Marissa. A twinkle lit her eye. "It looks as if things are about to get mighty interesting in good ol' Wadleyville, Ohio, U.S. of A. Yep, I'd say you're ripe for love all right."

"I have to get back to work," Marissa mumbled. She didn't want to talk about the embarrassing incident yet. Likely she never would. Besides, the man had come to buy a rose, probably for a girlfriend—though it was strange he hadn't wanted all the trimmings that came with the flower if it was for his girl. Still it was ludicrous for Marissa to think of any possibility of getting to know him better. Of getting to know him at all.

With grim purpose she grabbed a clipboard and pencil and headed toward her stock, determined to forget the existence of Antonio, the Latin charmer.

❧

Antonio breathed deeply of the smog-free air, appreciating its bracing freshness. According to one of the locals, he had missed two days of snow over a week ago. Antonio was relieved a thaw had hit shortly before he arrived in Wadleyville, though some stubborn patches remained in the shady areas. He doubted his car would have made it over icy roads. Standing on the sidewalk and staring across the sparse traffic of the two-lane street—sparse by L.A. standards—he eyed the quaint shops. Behind them lay gently wooded rolling hills, giving way to steeper hills in the not-so-far distance.

So far he didn't miss the hectic life associated with living in Los Angeles and was sure this small town would be a welcome change. If the townspeople were as charming as the woman he'd just left, the days ahead wouldn't be dull ones.

He turned and looked back at the little florist shop, with its lilac awnings over the carved ivory door and plate-glass window. The adjoining bridal shop had the same color awnings and door, and he wondered if Marissa managed both stores. Through the window displaying a variety of flower arrangements, he watched her talk with a plump woman, who seemed excited about something, using her hands expressively as she talked. Her delicate features solemn, Marissa offered little reply. Antonio took a moment to study her.

She wore her shoulder-length corn silk-colored hair in a nonfussy, sleek style, and her outfit matched the simplicity of the rest of her appearance. Of average weight and height, she reminded Antonio of his mother in stature. He couldn't see the color of her eyes from here, but he remembered them. Deep green, like the frond that had been in the vase of roses.

As though sensing his stare, Marissa looked his way. Feeling caught, Antonio smiled and inclined his head in acknowledgment, lifting the rose, as if in a toast. She said something to the woman and moved to the back of the shop.

Antonio left the window and walked to his car. Obviously he'd embarrassed her, both now and earlier. He'd been charmed by the girl and the brave way she handled the sugar mustache, but perhaps he'd laid his enthusiasm on a little thick?

Acting was in his blood, his family having had a long

association with it, and flowery phrases, though not meant to be insincere, were part and parcel of the life he'd left behind. Yet, in this small town, maybe such talk was considered artificial, and he should dispense with it if he were going to get along with others.

Hollywood had been his backyard, the stage his playground. While other kids shot hoops or rode bikes, his mother coached him hour after hour and worked to get him spots in commercials or bit parts in movies. After she'd battled a rare disease and lost, Antonio, a young sixteen, moved in with an aunt and did what he could to carry on his sluggish career. Once his aunt married and moved back to Spain, Antonio roomed with two other wanna-be actors and found himself a real agent. But he only received walk-on parts and minor roles for his trouble. The fact that he bore a striking resemblance to a popular Hollywood heartthrob, with the first name to match, didn't help boost his profession, though he'd changed his name at the time. No producer wanted two of the same. His agent even suggested that Antonio try out as the man's stunt double. But Antonio had argued that he was an actor, not a stuntman.

After receiving two important letters, each doing a significant part to change his life, he took back his original name and moved to this small town. He told himself that if his poor excuse for a career was washed up, before it could get a good foothold on Hollywood's ship of stars, then he would seek another source of income. One that was sure to pay off.

Two young girls across the street gaped at him, talking to each other and staring. Antonio was accustomed to such reactions and wanted to call out that he was *not* who they thought he was. But he only opened his car door and slid inside, carefully propping the rose on the passenger seat. He had business to take care of, and a long night lay ahead.

❧

Thick darkness covered Marissa's street by the time she pulled her silver compact into the detached garage, set the parking brake, and cut the ignition. She slipped the plastic ladybug on her key ring into her mouth, grabbed the two bulging paper bags of groceries, then headed for the house. Maybe Sherlock would forgive her for his late feeding when he smelled the gourmet cat food she'd brought him.

The Laughton-Paget wedding had given her nothing but problems. The young bride-to-be had stepped into her shop three months ago, sporting a nervous smile and a mantle of indecision. Six times she'd called since their initial meeting and made changes. Her last call ten minutes before closing time—with the request for a custom-made silk flower bouquet instead of the original real one—led Marissa to stay far after closing. With the wedding three days away, Marissa hoped Miss Laughton was at last satisfied with her choices.

Shifting the bags and crouching her head and shoulders lower, Marissa managed to get her hand to the key ring and pull it from her mouth to unlock the door. She frowned when the key stuck and jiggled it around. For the past two years she'd worked at restoring this house to better than livable conditions but had neglected to replace the forty-year-old lock. A project that just zoomed to number one on her home improvement list.

At last, the key turned, the latch gave, and the door swung open. She stepped inside, groceries still in her arms, and tried to free the key from the lock. Something furry swished past her ankles and out the door. She groaned.

"Sherlock—I'm selling you to the first taxidermist I meet!"

The cat raced across the street in a streak of brown and tan striped fur. The threat was empty. Marissa loved the mischievous tabby, and the old rascal knew it. Yet because Sherlock's former owner had removed his front claws, being out on the streets could be dangerous for him.

Marissa knew she had to go after the animal. She didn't want to spend the rest of the night worrying about the semi-defenseless Sherlock encountering a territorial dog or cat. She set the bags on the entry hall floor and closed the door behind her. The keys fell from the lock and plinked to the cement stoop.

She made a face at them before turning her attention to the dark dead-end, tree-lined road. It was lit by one lone street lamp near the turnoff and a smattering of porch lights. For the first time she wished her grandmother had bought a house in the midst of the brightly lit town instead of on its outskirts.

Obviously her neighbors were asleep. Their homes were dark. No—wait. The last house across the street at the end of the lane—two houses down with the woods behind it. A light shone from its kitchen window, above the row of over-grown shrubbery.

Chill bumps, having nothing to do with the cold air, danced across Marissa's flesh. That house had been empty for the past five months. When had it become occupied? Had a vagrant broken in? With the thick forest of trees nearby, starting only yards away from where the street ended, such an idea was feasible.

Marissa's next thought was lodged with the breath that jerked to a sudden stop in her throat. A tabby cat had jumped atop the house's window ledge and now brushed against its lit pane.

two

"Stupid, stupid cat," Marissa muttered. She pushed up her sleeves and made her way across the street then into the side yard of the supposedly abandoned house.

Sherlock sat on his haunches and looked her way as if surveying her, his royal subject. In no apparent hurry he began to lick his fur.

"No kitty treats for you tonight." Marissa judged the area between the long bush and the house. She hoped she was small and wiry enough to wriggle into the narrow gap. Wet twigs and leaves poked and scraped her as she shimmied into the confined space sideways. She sidestepped along the wall, using her hands on the vinyl siding to guide her.

"Ow! Make that no treats for a week," Marissa mumbled when something sharp jabbed between her shoulder blades. She stepped into a narrow clump of leftover snow that lined the building, the frozen particles oozing inside her pumps at the toes. She barely bit back a shriek at the contact.

Sherlock yawned and stretched out on the unbelievably narrow ledge, looking as if he planned to take a snooze. His golden eyes blinked disinterestedly at Marissa as she struggled to reach the window. The light scratches on her arms from the monster bush were beginning to itch. This had been a crazy idea. But she was more than halfway there and might as well continue.

At last she got to the window's edge and reached up for her cat. To her relief, Sherlock remained docile and didn't try to evade her groping hands when she fastened them around his warm, furry body. She lifted him off the ledge and drew him to her chest. "Dumb animal," she whispered. "If there *is* a vagrant inside, you're going to wind up getting us both in trouble. How am I supposed to get out of here while holding onto you?"

But, if there were a prowler, would he be so blatant with his approach? The light in the curtainless window acted as a beacon, announcing his presence to anyone around—anyone who was still awake, that is.

The window stood at eye level and was cracked open a few inches. Marissa wrinkled her nose at the fishy smell coming from within but couldn't resist a peek inside.

From the little she could see, two kitchen counters were cluttered with packing cartons—some open, some taped shut—and other boxes sat on a cardboard table in the center of the room. Near the porcelain sink, below the dirty pane, a can of tuna sat close by, the lid off. No wonder Sherlock had been drawn to this ledge.

Suddenly a man's face appeared at the window. Marissa let out a sound—between an inhaled scream and a gasp—and dropped the cat. Sherlock's back claws found their mark on her stomach before he raced out of the bushes.

❧

Antonio sped from the kitchen, the fork for which he'd been rummaging in the box still in his hand, and headed for the back door. When he first heard rustling in the bushes, he'd attributed it to a small woodland animal and hadn't paid much attention. Since the house was so close to the woods, he'd expected four-footed visitors to drop by from time to time. Hunger had driven him to search through the badly labeled cartons for his missing flatware. He'd found the electric can opener and removed the lid from the tuna but didn't locate something to eat it with until he looked in another carton. That's when he heard whispering outside and realized it was no animal that lurked in his bushes. His prowler was of the two-footed variety.

He'd seen only the top half of a face, but it was oddly familiar. With the way the eyes had widened, the "Peeping Tom" was as shocked to discover him there as he'd been to find a trespasser at his window at almost midnight.

Antonio took the three steps down the back porch, skipping the top and bottom stairs, and hurried around the side of the house—just as a woman in a skirt and sweater burst from the bushes. She raced for the street.

"Hold it right there!" Antonio yelled, raising the fork. He easily caught up to her and grabbed her arm with his other hand, pulling her around, intending to give her an earful. Instead he blinked. "Marissa?"

Her dark clothes were spotted with a few wet leaves, as was her hair. From the light of the kitchen window, Antonio watched her eyes widen. "Antonio?" she gasped. Her gaze went up to his other hand.

Realizing he still held his fork aloft, like a medieval sword, he lowered it to his side and released her. "What were you doing in my bushes?"

She backed up a step and stuttered something that sounded like, "Your—your lock is loose."

Antonio frowned. Why would she be interested in his locks? He'd left the window open, so clearly it *would* be unlocked. More important, why was she prowling around on his property in the middle of the night?

"My cat, I mean." She pointed down the street to a two-story yellow house with white trim. "I—I live there. Do you live here?"

By her jerky actions and addled words he could tell she was uptight. Maybe the whole incident was a misunderstanding. Since she lived close by, maybe she had simply been keeping an eye on things. She sure wasn't dressed to break into someone's home. And he didn't have much worth stealing—yet.

He considered dropping the subject, being neighborly, and inviting her inside for a cup of coffee. He'd have to dig through the boxes for filters and mugs, though. Then he remembered his resolve not to be too friendly.

He gave a short nod. "I moved in yesterday."

"Oh," she whispered with a small, uncertain shrug. She crossed her arms over her chest as though she were cold. "Well, um, welcome to the neighborhood."

"Thanks." Antonio didn't smile.

Marissa cleared her throat and looked at her watch. "My, but it's late." She backed away. "And I have to get up really early. Sorry for all the confusion." Before he could reply, she spun around and quick-stepped it across the street.

Antonio stared after her, watching as she reached her lit porch. She bent down, picked something up, then opened the door. Before she went inside, she looked over her shoulder in his direction. She paused, gave a little wave, then darted into her house.

Shaking his head, Antonio retraced his steps to the kitchen. He still couldn't believe she'd been scrambling around in his bushes this late at night and in a skirt. He thought back to her actions with the rose earlier that afternoon. Was her behavior always so quirky?

Grabbing his tuna and a quart-sized carton of chocolate milk from the refrigerator, he headed for the den. He sank to the lawn chair he was using until he could get some decent furniture and consumed his sparse dinner.

The local newspaper he'd purchased in town that morning caught his attention. Antonio decided to read some before he slipped into the sleeping bag he was temporarily using for a bed. The front headline leaped out at him:

CAT BURGLAR ON THE PROWL

He lowered the paper and stared thoughtfully into space.

❧

Once inside, Marissa leaned against the door, clutched her keys, and closed her eyes. Of all the places in Wadleyville for Antonio to move—it had to be on her street! Still, considering the downward slant this day had taken, the news shouldn't surprise her.

She groaned when she remembered her feeble excuse for being in his bushes—"Sherlock is loose"—and her idiotic behavior afterward. Their first encounter at the store and her powdered-sugar mustache were bad enough, but now he must think her an escapee from a mental ward!

Suddenly she remembered the bags of groceries, frowned, and picked them up. One was soggy on the bottom. Probably from the lime sherbet. Great. Green mush for dessert would just top off her day.

She put away the cold items, stuck a frozen waffle in the toaster, and poured some milk in a fluted glass. After finding the blueberry syrup in one of the bags, she retrieved her hot waffle, slid it onto a china plate, and settled down at the kitchen table.

Marissa had just started to eat when she heard a faint meowing at the side window. With a sigh she grabbed a can of cat food and emptied its contents into the bowl on the linoleum floor. She filled the other dish with fresh water then opened the back door. Sherlock trotted inside as though nothing were amiss and headed straight for his food bowl.

"Nice of you to drop by," Marissa said wryly. She crouched down and scratched him between the ears. He went on eating as if she weren't there. "It's for your own good I keep you inside, you silly cat. Learn to live with it."

After washing her hands and scratched arms, which were beginning to itch again, she resumed her meal. She picked up the old mystery movie she'd rented that morning and read the back of the video box while she ate, even though she'd read it twice already.

The ticking from the grandfather clock in the next room seemed to grow louder with each passing minute, making the house feel strangely emptier than usual. The clock was only one of many antiques Marissa had acquired over the years, though her goal was to fill every room with them. Her grandmother had left a number of antiques and this house to Marissa, and Marissa loved old-fashioned things. It was one reason she'd started her bridal shop, specializing in old-fashioned weddings.

At first, friends and family advised her against investing in such an unusual idea, certain the concept wouldn't succeed. But Marissa took a chance, a chance that paid off. Thanks to ads in the phone book and word of mouth, news about her "quaint little shop" spread, and she often had clients from neighboring towns seek her out to plan their weddings. Business boomed during the first two years, and when the small space next door became available to rent, she was able to acquire it for a florist shop. Marissa gained permission from the building's owner to hire carpenters to put in an entryway, adjoining the two shops. She'd also had the men knock out part of the wall at the rear so she could enter either shop from her back office.

Her ultimate goal was to own and manage a little wedding chapel, one fully equipped and able to provide all the necessary trimmings. She'd found the perfect spot to build on, near the edge of the woods on the other side of town.

She would hire a landscaper to plant climbing pink roses around the building, with a few almond-blossom and cherry-blossom trees out front and a lattice-worked white gazebo at the back. One day. . .

Marissa rose from the table and took her dishes to the sink. She rinsed them off and leaned closer to her window to stare out the chink between her cheery apple-and-grape print curtains. The light in Antonio's new home was still on.

As she'd done countless times that day, Marissa wondered about his reason for purchasing a single yellow rose. His actions were confusing, to say the least. At the shop he'd fairly bubbled over with enthusiasm and charm. Yet minutes ago, he'd been as cold and remote as an Alaskan glacier. An Alaskan glacier wielding a fork as a weapon. The switch from dashingly debonair to decidedly distant was unsettling. Of course, she could hardly blame him for his recent behavior, considering the circumstances.

Still, something about the secretive man intrigued Marissa. Why had Antonio moved to Wadleyville? Where had he come from? Was he a mystery just waiting to be solved?

The light in the window down the street went off, and Marissa pulled back from the curtain, deciding it might be wise to keep a close eye on her new neighbor. This time, from a much longer—and far less embarrassing—distance.

three

"He's here!"

At Linda's excited whisper, which carried over the office and probably into the store, Marissa lifted her cheek from her hand and turned from filling out an order. "Who's here?"

"That Antonio Banderas look-alike."

"Who?" Marissa wrinkled her brow.

"You know—that guy who moved to Wadleyville last week."

"Antonio's here?" Marissa asked faintly, feeling her pulse rate climb a notch.

Linda made a face as though Marissa were nuts. "Of course not! What would an actor be doing in a dumpy, out-of-the-way town like Wadleyville? It's his double who's out there."

"Whose double?"

"Antonio's double!"

"Antonio has a twin?"

"No—no! It's the guy from last week."

Marissa shook her head, uncertain if she was losing her sanity or if Linda was. She felt as though she were playing a similar reenactment of Abbott and Costello's "Who's on first?"

She raised her hands in surrender. "Okay. Come here. And whatever you do, please close that door first!" Her assistant did as she was told and clomped toward the desk in her thick-soled shoes. Marissa eyed her patiently. "Now tell me again slowly, and in English, please."

Linda rolled her eyes. "That guy—the one who bought the yellow rose—is in the shop. From several feet away I think he looks like Antonio Banderas, only younger." Linda raised her brows in a patronizing manner. "You do know who that is, don't you?"

"I've heard the name." Judy had taken her to see a few romantic comedies, but Marissa usually watched old movies so she wasn't up-to-date on a lot of current stars and didn't know what the actor looked like. She held onto her composure, but the news that her new neighbor had revisited her shop threatened to leave her tongue in a twirl. She'd barely seen him all week, except through her window when he left or arrived home in his ancient green Ford.

"Well," Marissa said, "if he's out there, then what are you doing in here?"

"He asked for you."

Composure flew out the window.

"For me?" Marissa squeaked.

"Yeah. And as much as I'd like to stick around, I have to go to that planning committee for the prom. You said I could take off early—remember?"

Marissa nodded, scarcely hearing Linda's words.

"I have some pictures of the actor in a magazine I'll bring next week. Then you'll see what I mean about that guy out there looking so much like him."

Linda grabbed her purse from off a nearby shelf, plucked a pack of gum from inside, unwrapped a piece, and fed the sugary stick into her mouth. "You know, Boss, it's really time you got out of the Stone Age and entered the real world."

"Good-bye, Linda," Marissa said firmly. Sometimes the girl could be so exasperating. "And incidentally his name is Antonio, too."

"Whose name?"

Not this again. Marissa nodded toward the door leading to the shop.

"Wow! No kidding? No wonder you were so confused."

Linda pulled the door open, peeked out and threw a grin over her shoulder. "I guess they couldn't be brothers then. Maybe cousins?"

"Maybe," Marissa mumbled, rising from her chair and leaving the office after the girl.

Marissa noticed Linda give their customer a curious look as she moved toward the door, and for a moment she feared Linda might actually query Antonio about his possible relationship to the actor. With relief she watched her go out and heard the shop bells ring.

The store was empty except for him. Marissa headed his way, determined to save as much face as she could. "What can I do for you today?"

He tried not to smile, but his lips twitched. She hadn't been eating powdered sugar pastries this time, but Marissa expected the worst. "Please tell me you didn't hear all that."

"Some of it." His eyes danced with amusement. "Permit me?" Suddenly reaching out, he rubbed her cheek with his thumb, his other fingers curled under her jaw. At the unexpected contact of his warm flesh, Marissa's heart felt as if it did a tango in her chest, dipping, twirling, beating fast. He pulled his hand away, showing her his thumb and the blue smear on it. "Sorry—no bandana today."

Marissa wished she could seep through the cracks between the tiles. "My pen's been leaking," she explained feebly and lifted her fingers to wipe away any ink that might be left. "Gone?" she asked.

He nodded. "I'm not related, by the way."

"Related?"

"To the actor."

"Oh." She shook her head and laughed. "You know—it seems that whenever we meet I'm not at my best, am I? More like at my absolute worst."

He grinned. "That's okay. I enjoy a bit of vaudeville to start and end my day." He opened his mouth, as if to say something else, then seemed to change his mind. "I came for a yellow rose."

"Another one?" Marissa asked before she could think. "She must be very special." The words were rapid, an attempt to cover her first blunder, but they sounded even worse—as though she were fishing to find out if he were attached.

He only smiled and moved toward the cooler a few feet away. She followed.

Opening the glass door, Antonio withdrew a vase and handed it to her. "Just one yellow rose," he explained. "Like last time."

Marissa eyed the pretty arrangement of yellow and blush-pink roses amid the baby's breath and fronds and gave a mental shrug, heading for the counter. He lived alone, had been in town a little over a week. Whom could he have met in such a short time that would warrant such treatment? Being in a small town, Marissa often heard news over the grapevine, whether she wanted to or not. And certainly, if an attractive newcomer like Antonio were dating one of the locals, Marissa would know by now. Unless maybe the romance was secret and no one had discovered it yet?

She walked to the back room to wrap the single flower in cellophane and a satin ribbon then rejoined him. "You might not know this, but flowers and their colors have certain meanings. For instance, a single red rose symbolizes romantic love, a way to say, 'I love you,' and a yellow rose symbolizes 'joy and gladness.' I've noticed, though, in the older books I've read that it's also been given the meaning of 'jealousy' or 'a love that is waning.'"

"Really?" He looked at the flower she held as though puzzled by her definition but handed her a five-dollar bill. "You seem to know your flowers."

"I've studied up on them." She lifted the clamp to slip the money into its slot in the register. "Floriography became popular in Victorian times when strict etiquette didn't allow women to express their feelings freely. So they did it coyly, using the silent language of flowers to express their sentiments to their admirers, and vice versa. Since I coordinate old-fashioned weddings, it helps to know these things."

She smiled and waited for him to change his mind about the flower color, sure that her explanation would prod him into doing so. "A white rose symbolizes 'worthiness and purity,' and a pink one, like this"—she motioned to the vase he didn't want—"symbolizes 'grace and sweetness' and 'perfect happiness.' I've also read it points to 'a secret romance.'" She eyed him intently as she said the last.

His expression didn't change. He pointed to the baby's breath. "What about that?"

"Innocence."

As though caught up in a game, he picked up a silk plant from a nearby shelf. "And this?" he said, pointing to the tiger lily among the white roses.

" 'I dare you to love me.' "

"What?" He looked taken aback.

"That's what the flower means." Marissa's cheeks warmed with her hasty explanation and the stunned look in his eyes. "It also symbolizes 'wealth and pride.'"

When the bells above the shop door rang, Marissa could have kissed the feet of the arriving customer for interrupting yet another awkward moment. Seeing her friend Judy walk through the door, Marissa changed her mind and wondered if she were destined to live the rest of her life in one long chain of embarrassing moments.

"Well," Judy said, eying Antonio. "Hel-lo again!"

"Again?" he asked, setting the silk plant down.

"I saw you leave the shop last Saturday," Judy explained. "And here you are again."

"Judy—Antonio," Marissa mumbled by way of introduction. "Antonio—Judy."

"No!" Judy looked as though she might fall over then peered at his face more closely. "Not the actor?"

"No, he's not an actor." Marissa hurried the explanation, noticing Antonio appeared uneasy. "He moved to town last week."

"We share the same neighborhood," Antonio added.

"Really?" A glint shone in Judy's eyes, making Marissa suspicious. "How interesting. And have you found a church yet?"

"I haven't had a chance to look."

"Well, you're welcome to visit ours. Services start at ten. We're the little white-shingled church up the road with the gray steeple and the sign out front that says, 'Wadleyville Fellowship.' You can't miss it."

Antonio smiled and held out his hand for Judy to shake. "The name is Antonio Ramirez, and I thank you for the invitation. I shall be honored to visit your church." He directed his gaze toward Marissa. "If I might have my change and my rose now?"

"Oh," she said, flustered. "Of course." She handed him the inappropriate-colored rose for his girlfriend and rushed to scrape his change together.

He inclined his head her way, his eyes sparkling. "I look forward to our next meeting—and to learning more about the silent language of flowers."

Marissa watched him exit the shop. She barely had time to draw a breath before Judy turned to face her. "What did he mean by that? Do you have a date with him?"

"Of course not!" Marissa stared at her. "What makes you ask such a crazy thing?"

"What's so crazy about it?" Judy lifted her hands, palms up. "As a matter of fact, I hope you do go out with him. You need to get out more. Holing yourself up in that old house isn't good for you. So did I hear right? He lives in your neighborhood?"

"Yes. In the old Kincaid place."

"You mean within walking distance—down the street?" Judy's words were followed by a satisfied smile. "God sure does work in mysterious ways!"

Marissa turned from her smug friend and picked up the vase to replace it in the flower cooler. "You're assuming an awful lot. I think he's spoken for. And I can't believe the way you just invited him to church."

"Why not?" Marissa could hear the shrug in Judy's voice as she followed. "If he's a Christian, he needs a church home—right? And if he isn't a Christian—well, we're encouraged to invite the unsaved to church, in hopes of helping them find God. So what's the problem?"

Marissa set the vase on the shelf, closed the door, and looked at Judy. "When you put it that way, nothing. But I know the real intent behind your invitation. You're hoping to pair us off."

"Hey, you could do worse than to date a drop-dead gorgeous hunk."

Marissa groaned. "Judy, do me a favor. I know you mean well, but please don't interfere. Besides, as I said, I think he already has a girlfriend. And I've told you countless times that I'm not looking for anyone."

"So maybe you don't have to look. Maybe God realized how stubborn you could be and delivered the man to your doorstep. Why else, of all available places to rent in town, would he have ended up on your street? And as to the supposed girlfriend—any man who looks at you the way

Antonio was doing just now can't be all that serious about another woman."

Marissa kept silent. She had no answer. Even if she did, chances were good that Judy would have a logical-sounding comeback, and Marissa decided she'd rather not know what it was.

❧

Antonio listened to the horrible clattering underneath his hood, which happened each time he drove the car up one of the hills that covered the area. Ever since he'd turned onto the road leading away from town the noise persisted. He couldn't afford to trade in his car—not yet—but he decided he'd better take it to a garage soon. The old Ford had carried him from California to Ohio, and it was probably past time to give her a tune-up—and more.

He patted the steering wheel. "Come on, old girl. You can make it a few weeks longer. Once I get the money to fix you up, that is."

Antonio had important business that wouldn't wait. He couldn't afford to be without a car for long.

Seeing a planter of purple flowers on a house stoop to his left, Antonio wondered what symbolic meaning they had and thought of Marissa. Not only was she cute, she was also intelligent. He felt a moment's remorse for not clearing up the fact that he was an actor, too, though not as good a one as the man he was constantly compared with; but maybe he'd been right not to speak. It was time to put that life behind him. A new opportunity beckoned. An exciting one that promised almost instant gratification, in return for a good deal of skill, courage, and determination on his part—if last Saturday night was anything to go by. At least his friend had warned him in advance of the pros and cons involved. But then Antonio was never one to say no to a challenge.

"Can you do it?" the plain-looking young woman asked, her brown eyes wide with hope.

Marissa stared at the sepia-toned photograph then smiled at her new client. "I don't see why not. The seamstress whose services I use is adept at making her own patterns from pictures of old wedding gowns. I'm sure it shouldn't be a problem for her to make a copy of your great-grandmother's wedding dress."

"Oh, it would be so great if she could!" The girl gave an awkward smile. "You see, I was adopted, and I just recently found my blood relatives. My adoptive parents are both dead—they were killed in a boating accident years ago—so this is important to me. Not that I don't like what you have to offer," she amended, glancing down at the thick book, open to a line drawing and a photograph of a gown from the twenties. "But I want to wear a wedding dress like the one my great-grandmother wore. In fact, I'd like to reenact the entire wedding—the flowers she carried, the music they played—everything. I have her diary. She was very detailed in describing it. My mom—my birth mom—is a hundred percent in favor of my idea."

"Of course." Marissa smiled to reassure her. "It's a wonderful idea. And that's what I'm here for, to help you realize your dreams. May I keep this?" She lifted the small photograph. "I could make a copy if you'd prefer, but the problem with that is the resolution wouldn't be as good. It might not show the detail of the lace or embroidery."

"I don't mind. Just"—the girl bit her lower lip, a worried frown creasing her brow—"please be careful with it. It's the only picture I have of my great-grandmother."

Under the girl's watchful gaze, Marissa slid the photograph into an envelope and placed it in the folder she was creating for her. "There. Safe and sound." Marissa offered another smile though the girl didn't seem mollified.

"Are you sure it'll be okay in there?"

"It'll be fine."

The door to BRIDAL DREAMS AND MEMORIES opened, accompanied by the ringing of bells, and a deliveryman came inside pulling a dolly with several boxes on it, varying from huge to medium-sized.

"Hello, Hank," Marissa said. "How are the wife and kids?"

The tall, lanky redhead gave her a wide smile, his teeth still stained from chewing tobacco during his high school rodeo years. "Can't complain. I need you to sign for this, and then I have orders to help you set it up in your office."

Set what up? Marissa eyed the dolly suspiciously then turned to her client. "I'm terribly sorry, Miss Reynolds, but I need to see to this. Gladys will help you and show you our full line of wedding accessories, as well as a book of floral arrangements you can choose from." She caught her assistant manager's attention and beckoned her, while picking up the Reynolds folder and rising from the table. "If you have any questions or concerns, please feel free to ask. I'll be in my office."

The young woman nodded, and the matronly Gladys approached with her winning smile and gregarious personality, which seemed to put Miss Reynolds instantly at ease.

Marissa handed the folder to Gladys then moved toward the deliveryman. "Okay, Hank—what's this all about?"

He grinned. "A late birthday present from your dad. I was told to deliver it and set it up."

Marissa withheld a groan, realizing what this meant. Even if the brown lettering on the boxes hadn't given it away, the fact that her father managed an electronics store, and Hank once worked for him, solved the puzzle. Marissa led the way to the back office and, at Hank's suggestion, cleared a space off her desk. Hank opened the first carton, confirming her fears.

"I don't know the first thing about using one of those," Marissa complained, her arms crossed. "And I'm not sure I want to."

The phone rang, and Marissa snatched it up.

"Hi, Sugar. Did it get there?"

"Daddy, you know how I feel about computers!"

"Before you throw Hank out the door on his ear, let me explain. You want to expand your business, but you operate the old way, and that takes time. This will help you utilize your time more efficiently. Trust me. It's easy to learn how to operate a computer. I've asked Hank to show you the basics and download some software I've included to make it even easier."

"Nice of the delivery service to loan out one of its employees for the day," Marissa mused.

Her dad chuckled. "Phil owed me a favor. I collected." A pause. "You know I only want to help in any way I can, don't you, Sugar?"

Marissa softened. "Yes, Daddy. I know." Since her mother died from a brain tumor years ago, her father was always doing things for Marissa, as if trying to make up for the loss. He still blamed himself that he never encouraged his wife to seek help earlier, when the dizziness and headaches started.

Marissa released a long sigh. "Oh, all right. I'll give it a try. But I can't promise I'll like it."

"That's all I'm asking. Just try it. I'll call you later tonight."

Marissa said good-bye and hung up the phone, surprised he hadn't taken the day off to come down here and put the thing together himself. He was so computer-oriented and always had the latest technological toys while Marissa was more like her old-fashioned late grandmother, her mom's mother.

"Hank, I hope your patience is pretty thick, because I'm probably not going to be the best of students."

He laughed as he pulled a huge rectangular device with buttons and what looked like miniature trap doors from a carton. "Not to worry. With ten kids to raise, I've learned the patience of Job." He set the ivory steel box underneath her desk. "Don't let me keep you from your work. This'll take awhile. I'll call you when it's ready."

Marissa hesitated. It wasn't that she didn't trust Hank, who was an usher at her church. Rather it was his comment that it could take awhile. Anything that took too long to set up couldn't be easy to use.

Holding back a sigh, she reentered the shop, first checking on Gladys and Miss Reynolds. Assured that all was going well, she moved into the adjoining florist area when she heard the bell ring. An eager young man entered, and Marissa helped him pick out an arrangement featuring cheery white daisies for his wife, who'd just delivered their first son. "Would you like me to make out a card?" she asked.

"No, I want to give them to her myself. Can I use one of those to write on, though?"

"Of course." Marissa moved the plastic container with the assortment of ten enclosure cards closer to him.

"Here." He thrust something blue her way. "Have a cigar!"

Marissa raised her brows in amusement at the candy cigar with "It's a boy!" printed on the wrapper. "Thanks." She smiled, slipping it into the breast pocket of her blue-gray silk blouse.

Once the man left, cradling the round glass vase, Marissa checked on Hank. He was messing around with numerous cables. Unable to work on her books or make any calls with Hank there, and with Miss Reynolds in obviously good hands, Marissa was left with little to do.

She rearranged shelves, mentally ran through a list of

last-minute errands for the Geraldi wedding that weekend and toyed with hiring another girl to work in the florist shop on the weekdays and add to her staff of four employees. Next week she planned to take Gladys with her to her wholesaler in Columbus and show her how to order the flowers, which were delivered by bus twice a week. It was time she gave her assistant manager more responsibility. As it was, Marissa couldn't consider taking any real time off since the shop wasn't yet able to run without her. She loved her work but needed a vacation from time to time as everyone else did.

Hours later the shop closed, but Hank was still tinkering on the computer. "Just a little longer. I'm downloading the software you'll need," he explained.

Marissa located a broom and swept the almost spotless white tiles that one of the girls had evidently cleaned already. As she moved past the flower cooler, her mind replayed her two encounters at this spot with the enigmatic Antonio. Vigorously she kept the bristles in motion, hoping to brush away any unwanted thoughts as well.

Her job finished, she went to the back workroom to put the broom away and noticed in the larger cooler a sympathy floral arrangement Linda had made to fill an order. The girl did have a gift, and her brother, Sam, was a big help in delivering flowers. Business had increased when the only other florist in the area closed five months ago. The local grocery store sold fresh flowers, too, though, so the added clientele in their small town hadn't been more than Marissa could handle. Her druthers would be to focus on weddings only. But she wasn't going to deprive the town of a need. Once she had her wedding chapel, then she would coordinate weddings exclusively and sell the floral shop.

Finally Hank called her into her office. He explained the

basics, showed her how to use what he called a "mouse," how to shut down the computer and turn it back on. He also told her how to get on the Internet. Then he gave her a thick manual to read and left her to face the computer beast on her own. Anything tagged with the name of a despised rodent didn't score points with Marissa.

She wrinkled her nose at the monitor, which displayed what looked like a news-story page. Settling down in her chair, she resigned herself to give it a go, as she'd told her father she would, and stared at the screen. A story about a week-old jewel theft in a neighboring town caught her eye. She moved the mouse to click on the blue link, as Hank had shown her, and read the article about a cat burglar who'd struck a home in a wealthy neighborhood last Saturday night. Suddenly she gasped, and her eyes widened as she reread the last few sentences.

The thief's calling card was a single yellow rose.

four

Marissa sat beside Judy and her husband on a middle cushioned pew, intent on the pastor's message. Judy lightly elbowed her in the side and nodded toward a pew in the next section, almost directly across from theirs. "He's here," she whispered. "It's a good sign."

Marissa looked at Antonio's profile in surprise. She hadn't expected him to come. Or was he here as part of his cover, to appear as a decent sort of guy, one nobody would suspect? Again her suspicions of him roused. Before church she'd bought a morning paper and hadn't been all that shocked to read that the cat burglar had struck in another close town last night, again leaving a yellow rose.

After the service Marissa watched Antonio approach Mike Shaeffer, the youth pastor who'd earlier made an announcement asking for additional help with the children's Easter play. Antonio seemed to be giving Mike a speech, as much as he was talking, but Marissa was too far away to hear. Curious, she moved closer to their aisle.

Mike sent an appreciative smile Antonio's way. "In that case I'd love your help! We meet on Wednesday nights at six."

"That shouldn't be a problem," Antonio said, and the two men shook hands.

"I'd like to help, too," Marissa jumped in. This would be a great opportunity to watch Antonio and try to find out more about him. Obviously her fellow church members didn't have any qualms about his sudden appearance in Wadleyville being connected with the recent thefts, though no one seemed to know anything about him when she'd offhandedly asked a few questions that morning. It was up to Marissa to check him out. All she knew about Antonio Ramirez was where he lived and that he came home very late last night.

"You, Marissa?" Surprise slackened Mike's features. "You want to help. With the play." His words came out as though double-checking to see if he'd heard her correctly.

"Sure." Marissa gave a little shrug. "Why not?"

"Maybe because you can't act," Judy whispered behind her, startling Marissa. She hadn't heard her friend come up; the spongy carpet muffled all sound.

Marissa grimaced. "It's not like this is for the academy awards or anything," she protested. "I've been wanting to help, by doing something for the church, other than just providing fresh flowers when needed. And this would be the perfect opportunity."

She kept her focus on Mike, ignoring Antonio, who quietly looked on. "Well, do you need the help, or don't you?" she asked.

Mike scratched the back of his neck. "Sure I do. Since two of our volunteers quit, we can use any help offered." His face cleared. "Thanks, Marissa. Your sacrifice will be rewarded."

"No, thank *you*, Mike." Marissa smiled for the first time. She glanced at Antonio and gave him an acknowledging farewell nod before making her exit. Judy wasn't far behind.

"What are you doing?" she asked Marissa as they stepped outside.

"I'm walking to my car."

"No, I mean, what was that business about helping with the play? You can't even stand up in front of the ladies' meeting without going three shades of pink. And that time you spoke up to give a testimony I thought you were going to hyperventilate."

"I'm a behind-the-scenes person," Marissa countered. "And helping with this play is behind the scenes."

"Yes, but you don't have any experience in drama. You haven't done any acting."

"I was a lamb in the Christmas play."

"That was fourth grade, and the teacher made you do it. Besides, you broke out in hives afterward."

"Only because of that awful scratchy wool from the costume."

"Marissa." Judy stopped walking and grabbed her arm, pulling her about. "What's behind this? Why the sudden interest in something you've avoided like moldy leftovers up till now?"

Before she could answer, Antonio walked past. "I'll see you on Wednesday," he said with a grin, holding his hand up in a wave as he moved toward his car.

"Yeah, see you," Marissa replied.

Judy let out a soft giggle. "Light's beginning to dawn. Would your sudden interest in the play have anything to do with a drop-dead gorgeous Latin who's also volunteered his time? Of course." She answered her own question with another giggle, slapping her palm to her forehead in a mock gesture. "It must be!"

"Judy—it's not what you think."

"Hey, Jude!" Judy's stocky husband, Glen, called out from a car three spaces away. "If we don't want to stand in line at the restaurant, we'd better get a move on. Later, Rissa."

Marissa waved back. "By the way, how'd Glen get so sunburned?"

"He fell asleep in his boat when he went fishing—but stop trying to change the subject," Judy said lightly. "It's not going to work. I'll be by the shop first thing Thursday to hear more about your time together with Antonio."

Watching Judy walk away, Marissa felt only a slight twinge of guilt for not telling her friend she'd be absent from the shop most of Thursday morning.

Antonio turned his head and looked out over the sanctuary at the many exuberant, giggling faces. He couldn't remember ever being around so many kids this young, not since his own schooldays. Twenty first-through-seventh graders must have been there. The children sat on pews, some perched at the edges as though eager. A few sat cross-legged and looked bored. Two of the older girls waved stapled-together scripts in front of their faces like Southern belles with fans.

"Hey, Jeff," Antonio heard a small tyke whisper nearby. "Ain't that the dad from the spy movie we saw?"

"Naw," another boy said. "He just looks like him. My daddy said his name is Mr. Ramirez. He told us last Sunday after church that he was coming tonight."

"Oh." The child sounded disappointed. "That's too bad, 'cause I was gonna ask him if he had any spy gadgets that would make Wendy disappear."

Antonio couldn't help the soft chuckle that shook his chest. His gaze went to another group of kids when one boy rolled up his script and bonked the head of an older boy in front.

"Hey!" The red-faced kid rubbed his scalp and cast a vengeful look at the smiling culprit behind him. "Cut it out, Chris. Or I'm telling Mom when we get home."

"All right, boys, enough." Mike took a place at the front of the sanctuary. "We have a genuine Hollywood actor with us tonight—though let me make it clear from the start that he's *not* the dad from the spy movie. He's going to help us with the play and, I hope, take over the directing since I was so bad at it." A few snickers met his comment. "I want you boys and girls to be on your best behavior for Mr. Ramirez."

When Mike first introduced him, Antonio noted the surprise that swept across Marissa's face and the sharp look she threw his way. He should have cleared up the fact to Marissa that he was an actor, too, but he'd let it slide. At her somber stare he wished he hadn't.

Stepping behind the podium, he focused on the sea of faces before him and delivered a short spiel designed to tell about himself and get the children excited about the story. He'd read the script earlier—an original twist on the Easter story, as seen through the eyes of a modern-day little girl whose older brother died half a year earlier. Jesus' last days on earth and His glorious resurrection were interspersed throughout the contemporary scenes. Antonio wondered if the theme was a bit heavy for such young ones to pull off. But Mike had assured him the kids could handle it and had been doing so for three weeks; further, his wife had written the play so he was convinced it would be all right. Antonio was willing to work hard, but he hoped Mike knew what he was doing.

Marissa handed out scripts to the children who'd left theirs at home, and they did a read-through of the first few scenes.

"Chris," Antonio finally said, "have you ever noticed something about actors on TV? They usually don't have jawbreakers in their mouths when they say their lines. It would make their words difficult to hear."

"No candy in the sanctuary, period, Chris," Mike inserted, pointing to the back of the church. "In the trash—now. You know better."

Realizing some of the kids had to leave early, having been reminded of that fact five times by a small boy wearing thick, black Poindexter glasses, Antonio announced they would skip a few scenes. They moved to the part with Mary Magdalene and the angel, since those two girls had said they wouldn't be able to come the following Wednesday. Antonio nodded to the tall redhead to begin her lines.

She looked at her script and squinted her eyes. With a jubilant smile on her face, she swept one arm to the heavens and announced, "Behold! You will not find Him here. For He is a raisin from the dead."

Several boys snickered loudly. Antonio shot Marissa a look over the girl's head; she was having a hard time keeping a straight face, too.

"Cindy," Mike said patiently. "I believe that's supposed to be 'He is arisen from the dead.'"

"That's not what my script says, Pastor Mike."

"Let me see that." Mike walked toward the front and took the proffered script. "Why, this has been tampered with!"

More snickers could be heard from the back of the church, and Mike spun around.

"Chri–i–is!" He and the angel, Chris's older sister, exclaimed.

Chris had to sit on the front pew for discipline, and the rest of practice went almost without a hitch. The shy girl who played Mary kept mixing up her lines, and Mike finally said it was time to go, encouraging the children to practice every spare moment they could.

Antonio wondered what he'd gotten himself into. He hoped he had the ability to direct these modern-day "Little Rascals," as everyone seemed to think. He hunkered down to slide his copy of the script into the folder he'd brought from home.

"So you're a Hollywood actor." Marissa stood near his elbow.

Antonio looked up to catch a mistrustful glint in her eye. "I was. I gave it up before coming to Wadleyville."

Marissa nodded vaguely, as though she didn't really hear his words but had something to say. "You could've said something when the subject was brought up at the shop. Why didn't you say anything when I told Judy you weren't an actor?"

"I'm sorry. You're right. I should have mentioned it."

She huffed out a little breath. "No. Never mind. I'm the one who should be apologizing. I have no idea why I said all that just now. You certainly don't owe me any explanations. I don't even know you that well."

"We could remedy that." He gave her a tentative smile and stood to his feet. "Will you come with me to Lucy's Café for a bite to eat? Mike and his wife are going, too."

Marissa hesitated, and Antonio thought for a moment she might agree; but she shook her head. "I have a lot to do tomorrow morning. I need to call it quits early."

"You sure? It's only eight o'clock."

"Yes, really—I'm sure. I have to be at the shop earlier than usual, and I have some chores I need to do tonight. Believe me, if I could, I'd join you guys." She fished her keys out of her purse, snapped it shut, and looked at him. "Maybe another time?" She hooked the purse strap over her shoulder.

"Okay. I'll walk you to your car."

"Oh, you don't have to do that," she said a little too quickly. "I'm parked just outside the door at the back."

"Then the walk won't be a long one." Antonio moved ahead of her through the door leading into the dark narrow hallway that wrapped around the sanctuary. He pushed down the silver bar to open the back exit door. Last stages of twilight fell across the wet parking lot, obscuring color and making it difficult to see. High branches of sycamore trees on the other side of the fence shadowed the vehicles. "I don't mind," he added, holding the door open for her. "Besides, my car is parked next to yours."

"So it is," Marissa murmured, staring at the two cars. She gave him a feeble smile. "Well, in that case, how can I refuse?"

Antonio sensed her tension and sought an easy topic for the short distance to their cars. "Those MacGrady children sure have talent, don't they? But that boy Joe is a ham. The way he stood up to take a bow after delivering his lines—then pretended to lose his balance and fall headfirst on the carpet.

And Chris"—Antonio shook his head in amused disbelief—"I hope we don't have any more trouble with that one."

"Chris is Chris," Marissa said with a shrug, as if that should explain everything. "And Joe got his comical ways from their father. Hank's a deliveryman by day and a devoted father and husband by night. But during any special events he plays the part of a clown."

"Really?" Antonio chuckled. "That would explain it."

They had reached their cars. Antonio stood near the passenger side of his car and watched Marissa slip her key into the lock, open the door, then look at him. "Well, I guess I'll be going."

"Marissa, about the MacGrady girl, the one with the role of Mary. She needs a bit of coaching, and I noticed she seemed more comfortable around you than around Mike or me or even Sandy. Would you mind working with her one on one? Mike gave me full rein, as far as the directing goes, which is why I'm even bringing it up."

Doubt clouded her eyes. "There's something you should know, Antonio. I can't act. When I was a little girl, I froze up on stage, so I'm probably not the one to help you with Genna. I'm sorry." She slid behind her steering wheel and glanced up again, as though she wanted to say more but wasn't sure what.

Antonio resisted his first inclination to ask why she'd volunteered to help with the dramatization in the first place and gave her what he hoped was an understanding grin. "That's okay. You and Genna can help each other."

"What do you mean?" Her words came out stiff.

"The adults are participating in the play, too. Mainly as extras, to help coach the little ones and keep an eye on them. Mike's wife had the idea. The truth is, the play was written for more than we have on hand, so we need several adults to take on roles as extras."

"I can't! I—I mean—" Her knuckles turned white as she clutched the wheel. "Maybe I can do something backstage to help out instead?"

"Relax. You won't have a speaking part. You'll just blend in with the crowd."

She gave a half smile. "I'll think about it." She slid her key into the slot. Her engine turned over and started with a muffled roar. " 'Bye." She slammed her door and put the compact into a hasty reverse as though she were afraid to stick around any longer.

Antonio watched until her car turned right at a nearby stop sign. Again he wondered why Marissa would volunteer for something she obviously didn't enjoy. He slipped behind the wheel of his Ford and slid the key into the ignition. The whirred groanings of the engine trying to turn over sounded as if the ancient metallic beast were in pain. After three attempts Antonio shut his eyes and let his head fall forward to hit the steering wheel.

The need for quick funds just topped his priority list. He saw only one remedy to get the money to fix his car or buy a new one, to keep up with house rental payments, and to pay the bills. But keeping weekends open might prove to be a problem in his getting a day job. Antonio smiled. At least he had Saturday nights, though the benefits from that profession had only just begun to pay off. What he received in return for his hard work helped, but he would need more money in his savings account soon. If he were to get his car worked on, the bill would probably take a healthy chunk out of his funds.

But at least he had Saturday nights.

five

"He is definitely up to something," Marissa mumbled, watching Antonio leave her shop after his fourth visit there.

Despite Marissa's awkwardness at having Antonio catch her near his bushes again last night—at least this time she had produced the stubborn Sherlock so had felt a little more justified to be on his lawn after sundown. Yet yesterday's incident was nowhere near as embarrassing as the first, when she'd literally been stuck in his bushes. So after Antonio sauntered into her store this afternoon, just as Marissa was about to take a lunch break, she told the new girl, Kaitlan, that she'd wait on him before leaving. She hadn't been all that surprised when they'd gone through what Marissa now called "the ritual of the yellow rose."

With an hour to kill she planned to follow Antonio and see to whom he gave the flower, if the rose was indeed for a girl. Marissa was fairly certain it wasn't. Everyone at her church thought Antonio was the best thing to come along since gourmet microwave dinners, but Marissa wasn't so sure. She had almost convinced herself he was the cat burglar who'd struck neighboring towns—twice now. He fit her portfolio, anyway.

From mystery movies she knew every good detective had a modus operandi for charting their suspects, and so did Marissa. Antonio was slim but athletic—which would make it easy for him to climb trees and buildings silently and with ease. He seemed to favor dark clothing—a must for any cat burglar—and was secretive about a number of things, including where he spent his Saturday nights. Add to that the weekly yellow rose, the calling card of the cat burglar, and Marissa was sure she had her man.

Once she saw his lithe form move past the plate-glass window, she darted into her office, grabbed her purse and sweater, and hurried out the shop door. On the sidewalk she looked in the direction she'd seen him go.

There was no sign of him.

Frustration propelled her steps as she half-walked, half-ran along the cement walk. Four stores ahead, two women strolled along, each holding the hand of a little girl who toddled between them. On the road, cars of every color but forest green whizzed past on their southward and northward journeys. A pickup truck chugged by, emitting a cloud of gray smelly exhaust from its tailpipe and making Marissa grimace and want to cough. She looked across the street to spot a man entering a clothing store, but he didn't fit Antonio's description either.

Marissa reached the end of the sidewalk. Rather than step off the curb and hurry across the street to the other sidewalk that fronted another string of shops, she turned the corner and walked several yards. Seeing no one, she peeked around the brick wall and scanned the short, narrow alley her shop shared. Besides a raccoon sitting on its haunches atop a green dumpster, his ringed bushy tail twitching when his black-masked eyes caught sight of her, no other sign of life was evident.

"Latin charmer, where are you?" she muttered.

"Looking for someone?"

Marissa wasn't sure which jumped higher—her heart from her chest or her shoes from the cement. Spinning around, she faced Antonio. Her tongue seemed to be inconveniently glued to the roof of her mouth.

His high brow wrinkled in bemusement, and he cast a

glance down the alley. The raccoon darted away and up a tree. Marissa wished she could join it.

"Were you looking for me?" he asked.

Marissa forced her brain to think up a logical response. "Yes. You forgot your change," she blurted then wished she could have bitten her tongue. That was logical?

The corners of Antonio's mouth turned upward in a slight smile, but his expression still showed confusion. "It was only a nickel."

"I—" Marissa opened her purse and dug at the bottom for the coin. "Here," she said at last, handing over five pennies. "If Abraham Lincoln could walk a few miles to return a penny to a customer, I can walk around the block with five." She smiled, but it felt stiff. Her lips seemed stuck to her teeth.

He continued to stare at her as though she'd just stepped off the Looney-Tunes train. Well, she was acting like a cartoon nut, so who could blame him?

"It's really not necessary," Antonio said, making no move to take the coins. "What I need is a phone. My car won't start, and I have important business to attend to."

Marissa thought fast, her gaze going to his hand and the yellow rose she'd wrapped in cellophane. "I can drive you wherever you need to go. I'm on my lunch break now."

"No, that's okay. If I could just use your phone, I'd appreciate it."

"Sure." Marissa kept the bright smile on her face though she wanted to groan. How was she supposed to trail him in a taxi? Well, she could try, but by the time he called and one arrived, her break would probably be half over. "Sure you don't need a lift?"

"Thanks, but my business will take longer than a lunch break."

"Okay." Disappointed that her attempt to trail him had

failed, Marissa walked with Antonio back inside Sweet Scents. Ignoring Kaitlan's surprised reaction at seeing her return with an earlier customer, she pulled the counter phone around so her suspect could use it.

ক

Antonio punched in the number to make arrangements for a taxi, all the while wondering why Marissa was acting so strange this time. Ever since he'd met the cute blond she'd been a mystery difficult to unravel.

She remained behind the counter, straightening pens and pencils in their holder by the register, sweeping unseen particles from the glossy counter into her palm, rearranging the mini enclosure cards in the upright plastic container. If Antonio didn't know better, he would think she was eavesdropping on his conversation with the cab company. She wouldn't meet his eye but didn't seem in a hurry to leave either. Didn't she say she was on a lunch break?

Her frond-green eyes suddenly met his, and a faint blush colored her cheeks. She hastily lowered her gaze and went back to straightening the already neat counter.

While he was put on hold, he wondered if turning down her offer for a ride had wounded her and if that was why she seemed so uneasy. Maybe she was only trying to make amends for refusing to go to dinner with him after play practice—or for last night when he discovered her scrounging around in his bushes again. At least this time she had produced a tiger-striped cat, which she immediately clasped to her chest before uttering a hurried good-bye and making a beeline for her home. Yet maybe, deep down, she wanted to be friends and was too shy to say so.

The arrangements for his cab made, Antonio hung up the phone.

"Everything okay?" Marissa asked.

"A cab will be here in about fifteen minutes. They're busy today. It seems there's a convention going on near Columbus."

"Oh." She darted him a hesitant smile. "You're welcome to stay in the shop while you wait, of course. I have a chair in the back, if you'd like to sit down."

"Thanks. I'm fine."

"Can I get you anything? A soda or something? We have a small fridge in the office. I bought it for those days when I'm too swamped to go out and eat lunch. Lately that's been every day—except today, of course." Her laugh seemed forced.

To Antonio, it sounded as though she were trying to fill in what remaining time they'd be together with as many words as she could pack into the minutes.

"There is something you can do for me," he said after staring at her awhile, watching as she broke a roll of dimes against the open drawer of the register. There wasn't much else she could do to the counter.

"Yes?" She lifted her head to send him an inquiring look.

"Have dinner with me tomorrow night."

She froze, holding the cracked-open roll of dimes in midair a few inches above the drawer. Some of them plinked into the almost-empty coin compartment. The sound seemed to bring her back to her senses. She dumped the rest of the coins in, closed the register drawer, and looked at him. "Okay."

Her calm, unflustered response was as unexpected as a summer snowstorm. She was a contradiction of emotions and actions, and Antonio looked forward to trying to sort them out, to getting to know the real Marissa Hughes. Such a prospect would certainly be well worth his time.

❧

A few minutes after Antonio left the shop, Judy bustled through the door. "I thought I'd save you a trip and pick up those silk flowers for the LaRue wedding. The cake is baked, and I'm almost ready to frost it."

Marissa nodded and headed to her office, plucking up the tagged bluish-purple silk violets the bride-to-be had specified she wanted to decorate the tiered bridal cake. Marissa thought the young woman's choice of flower—depicting faithfulness, love, and loyalty—was a good one to top a wedding cake. Before she left the office, her gaze flitted to the cover of the celebrity magazine Linda had brought that morning. While Marissa could see striking similarities between the famous actor and Antonio, she also saw marked differences. For instance, her Antonio's jaw was a tad more square, his nose a bit narrower, and his eyebrows were shaped a little differently and weren't quite so thick. Also, his eyes were a lighter brown. Sienna brown almost. They seemed gentler, too, though they also gleamed with hidden fire, hinting at un-explored passions.

Her Antonio? Unexplored passions? What on earth was she thinking?

She could feel her face growing hot, as if she'd just exited a steam bath. Judy must have noticed because a huge smile lifted her plump cheeks.

"My, my—I'd sure like to know what you have back there that has you coming out of your office, blushing like one of your roses."

Marissa handed over the violets then fanned her face with her hand. "It's hot in here. Don't you think it's hot in here? Of course, I've been running around a lot today."

"Uh huh. Didn't I see Drop-Dead Gorgeous leave the shop a few minutes ago?"

Marissa sighed, realizing her ploy hadn't worked. "Will you please stop calling him that? And, yes, he came by for another yellow rose."

"In—ter—esting." The way Judy drew out that one word gave it more meaning than it held.

"What's so interesting about it? After all, I'm the only florist in town right now. Where else would he go?"

"Right." Judy nodded slowly. "But I wouldn't be at all surprised if he asked you out sometime soon."

The betraying heat scorched Marissa's face again.

Judy's eyes widened. "He did, didn't he? And you weren't going to tell me."

"Judy, it's not like you think—"

"Just answer me this—did you accept? Are you going out with him?"

Marissa hesitated. "Yes, but let me explain—"

"Yes, yes, yessss!" Judy pumped her fist into the air with each word. Marissa half expected her friend to discard her flour-spotted apron, whirl it over her head, and do a victory dance next.

Leaning over the counter, she grabbed Judy's thick wrist. "Will you please listen to me?"

"I'm all ears," Judy said, her grin close to reaching both of them.

"Wonderful. Well, unstop those ears completely because this is important. I have a good reason for accepting Antonio's dinner date, and it's not what you think." Marissa sorted out the best way to explain. She hadn't told anyone about her suspicions yet, but if she were to tell someone, that someone would be her best friend. She decided to come straight out with it. "Judy, I think Antonio may be a cat burglar."

Her friend stared at her a few seconds then burst out laughing.

Marissa frowned. "That wasn't meant to be funny. If you knew what I did, you wouldn't be laughing."

Judy worked to keep the smile off her face. "And what is

this fount of evidence you possess, oh, Madame Detective?"

"I'll show you." Marissa marched to her office, plucked up the latest news story she'd printed out with her computer printer and returned to the counter. "There!" she said triumphantly, handing over the paper. "Read it for yourself."

Judy skimmed the article and handed it back, her expression deadpan. "So what?"

"What do you mean 'so what'? Isn't it obvious? Look here." Marissa pointed to a paragraph on the paper. "His calling card is a single yellow rose. Ring any bells?"

"Just because Antonio buys yellow roses doesn't mean he's a cat burglar, Marissa. Some people prefer yellow. Not everyone is as knowledgeable about floriography as you are."

Marissa drew her brows together. "Okay, then what about this?" She pointed to another paragraph. "It says here that the thief struck Bolton. Well, that's where I heard Antonio tell the cab driver he wanted to go today. Bolton."

"Big deal. I went there recently, but that doesn't make me a cat burglar either. But while we're dissecting this article, let me bring something else to your attention." Judy scanned the paper and pointed to a line near the bottom. "There. Read that."

"The two break-ins are similar in that they both occurred on a Saturday night and—"

"Right!" Judy said, without letting Marissa finish. "The date on here is last week's. But you said Antonio has been to your shop four Saturdays in a row for yellow roses, today included. The numbers don't add up."

Marissa frowned. "Maybe he got sick and had to call off one of the burglaries. Come to think of it, I didn't remember seeing him come home last Saturday, so maybe he was there all along."

"Or maybe that overactive imagination of yours is trying to find any excuse it can to avoid regarding Antonio as a prospective date." Judy's expression softened, and she laid a freckled hand on Marissa's forearm. "It's understandable, Rissa. Grant hurt you, and you're afraid to get involved with someone else. Anyone can sympathize. But don't throw a good thing away just because you're afraid to try again. Antonio is warm and funny and great with kids. All the single women at our church almost drool when he walks through the door—but he only sees you. His eyes light up only when you're around. So stop trying to play Holmes with your Sherlock, before you wind up making a big mess of things."

"But what about the rose?" Marissa argued, not wanting to admit how close Judy's well-meaning arrow had come to her love-punctured heart. "He asks for the same thing every time and doesn't want any extras."

Judy picked up the bunch of silk flowers from the counter where she'd put them. "Maybe they're for his mom. Maybe she has a thing for yellow roses, and he takes one to her when he goes to visit for dinner on Saturdays. Who knows?"

Marissa doubted that Antonio was the saint Judy painted him, but she didn't offer further arguments.

Judy let out a weary sigh. "You're going to keep on with this silly sleuthing of yours and ruin everything, aren't you? You just won't quit." With a sad shake of her head she walked to the door. "I'll see you later. I need to get back to work on that cake."

The shop bells announced Judy's exit. Spotting a stray flower that had fallen from the bunch, Marissa went around the counter and squatted down to pick up the lone violet.

Love. Faithfulness. Loyalty.

No one had ever given Marissa such cherished promises. Grant had offered them, but his words were insincere. One night, two weeks after their engagement almost a year ago, Marissa found him at his apartment with an old schoolmate of hers, a girl she'd asked to be one of her bridesmaids. And they weren't discussing the wedding.

Looking back, Marissa wondered how she'd never seen the signs. His roving eyes when they were in a room with beautiful women, his lame excuses for not coming to see her days in a row, his cancellation of their ice-skating dates. At least she was thankful she'd learned the truth before a marriage could take place, but that hadn't prevented numerous nights of sleeping with a wet pillow, salty from her tears.

Marissa stood hastily. It did no good to think about that lowlife. She had bigger fish to fry. Namely, the capture of one enigmatic cat burglar. Since the solitary person in whom she'd chosen to confide hadn't believed her, she doubted the law would either. She must scrape up enough evidence to ensure police interest and involvement. And Marissa had the perfect bait.

six

After church on Sunday, Marissa played tug of war with the lock and key, finally letting herself inside her house. She slipped off her pumps, the cool floor feeling good under her stocking feet, and fixed herself a toasted bacon, cheese, and tomato sandwich. While she spread on mayonnaise and heaps of shredded lettuce, her gaze wandered to the kitchen window.

Often these past two weeks, the cheery-curtained pane had drawn her like a tot to a new cartoon, compelling her to stare outside and try to discern any signs of life at Antonio's place. Her new neighbor hadn't been at church today. And last night she'd given up watching for his headlights to appear, finally dropping into bed at three in the morning, after the late-night mystery movie was over. Sheer determination not to miss church services was all that enabled her to roll out of bed this morning, with gritty eyes and a foggy mind. She'd even had to skip breakfast to make it on time.

Moseying over to the window, Marissa crunched into her sandwich and chewed, watching the house down the street. Suddenly the front door opened, and Antonio stepped onto the porch, clad in black gym pants and a matching tank top that showed off a set of well-defined biceps. Marissa managed to swallow. Didn't the man know it was forty-one degrees outside for goodness sake? Or did those tanned, nut-brown arms never get cold?

He did a few stretches and deep knee bends. Then, picking up a small backpack from a nearby chair and looking around, as though to be sure no one was watching, he headed off the porch and into the nearby woods.

Now what was he up to?

Marissa wasted no time and slid back into her pumps. Lunch still in hand, she grabbed her keys off the table, hurried outside, and locked the front door. Taking another bite of her sandwich, she waded through a patch of Virginia bluebells on the outskirts of the woods. Many pale pink clusters of buds were on their way to opening and changing into the graceful soft-blue, trumpet-shaped flowers. They were now at what Marissa thought of as the "baby colors stage"— when the flowers were both pink and blue and some a shade in between.

As she entered the woods and found the path, this morning's message from the Gospel of Matthew replayed in her mind, giving her added incentive. "But understand this: If the owner of the house had known at what time of night the thief was coming, he would have kept watch and would not have let his house be broken into." Marissa understood the true context of the verse and the pastor's message that followed, but at the same time she considered the verse a directive from God—that she was to continue her investigation of the secretive Latin. It was up to her to protect her town, not to mention her own material possessions. It was up to her to keep watch.

The chill breeze made her glad for her fuzzy gray sweater, though she wasn't thrilled with her morning's choice of a full skirt—as opposed to how wonderful a pair of woolen slacks would feel right about now. And comfortable shoes with no heels. How could a dirt path have so many pebbles and sticks? She stepped along as quickly as she could in her pumps, trying to catch sight of Antonio. When the path forked, she decided to take the right lane since the trees were denser there. Had he buried his stash somewhere in the woods? Or was he meeting someone to make the trade of money for the jewelry? Maybe the jewelry was in the backpack.

The forest was bigger than Marissa had thought it would be. She had lived in her little yellow house for years but had never set foot in these woods. As she took in the many lush pines and tall budding hardwoods, she wondered why. Carpets of colorful wildflowers lifted their delicate petals in the sunnier areas, while three-petaled white trillium nestled in the shade. The shrill call of a cardinal's "Cheer! Cheer!" sang in the damp air, blending in with the clinking of her key chain. What sounded like a stream from somewhere nearby gurgled a melody through the close-standing trees. The scenery was lovely, and Marissa would have enjoyed it more—if she'd been dressed for a hike.

She took a few twists in the path, each time thinking she heard something ahead. Endless twigs from prickly bushes or pine needles grabbed at her clothes and hair. Finally Marissa decided she should return to the wider path. On doing so, she walked farther along and up a gradual slope until she saw another split in the lane and decided to take the one that branched left.

She tripped over a knobby piece of wood protruding out of the ground and just caught herself from falling face down on the hard-packed soil by grasping onto some bushes. Soon she was hopelessly lost, and she hadn't even glimpsed Antonio. She was beginning to think the man must be part wood sprite. No, he was too well built to be a figment of one's imagination. A gypsy then. How else could he blend into the trees so well without making a sound, as though he'd become one with the forest? She hadn't been that far behind, to lose him so completely.

Spotting a fallen, decayed log ahead, Marissa gratefully

took a seat and slipped out of her pumps. At that moment she didn't care about catching her nylons on the rough bark. She dug the burning balls of her feet deep into the cool, wet grass and looked at the ruined sandwich. The wheat bread was speckled with dirt and little green things. Wrinkling her nose, she laid it on the log beside her. Maybe one of the woodland animals had a taste for bacon.

Leaning forward, she propped her elbows on her knees and rested her chin on her fists. She pondered her dilemma. The witty detective Nick Charles never ran up against such obstacles in all the *Thin Man* movies she'd seen—and he never would've gotten himself lost. Of course, Nick did have the aid of his intelligent dog Asta, who could even do flips. Whereas Marissa had only a fat cat named Sherlock who liked to snooze on her neighbor's window ledge at the most embarrassing times of the night—when Antonio was home.

Sleuthing looked a lot easier on film than it was in real life. Marissa felt more like Nick's wife, Nora, who often found herself in a pickle in her desire to help her detective husband. The chic woman always appeared fresh, though, and wouldn't end up with bits of vegetation stuck to her sweater or in her hair.

Frowning, Marissa plucked a few tiny pointed leaves from her fuzzy sleeve. She hoped none of this was poison ivy.

Hearing the soft pad of footsteps come close, she suspected the worst. She would almost prefer to see a black bear or a sharp-toothed fox. A rustle of bushes, a snap of a twig, and her worst fears were realized. Antonio appeared, the expression on his face worthy of being captured on film. Too bad she didn't have a camera.

&.

Antonio closed his mouth and shook his head slowly. He was beginning to doubt if he'd ever figure this woman out. Bits of leaves and small twigs stuck out of Marissa's usually sleek hair, which appeared as if it had been caught on overhead branches. Her nice clothes were no better off—and whoever heard of wearing shoes like that to hike? His gaze went to a dirty, half-eaten sandwich sitting beside her and a set of keys next to it, and he lifted his eyebrows in mystified amusement. At least the keys explained the clinking sounds he'd heard earlier.

"Do I want to know?" he asked.

Pink colored her shiny face, and she shook her head. "Just can you please get me out of this jungle? I'm lost."

Lost? He was beginning to wonder if she'd lost her mental faculties as well, but he offered her a hand. "Sure."

She slid into her shoes, wincing as she did, and took his hand. He hoisted her upward, and she stumbled and fell against him.

Antonio caught a whiff of her flowery-vanilla-sweet perfume before she pushed herself away from his chest. He pulled a small twig from her hair, gaining her shocked attention. For a moment he stared into her wide green eyes then took her hand again.

"Come on. Let's get you back home."

Marissa's palm felt clammy in his, but Antonio didn't let go. Together they walked through the shady hemlocks and cedars until he came to the small clearing where he'd sat for awhile, looked over his notes, and grown meditative. Marissa gasped.

Antonio looked at her. "You okay?"

Her focus was on the narrow stream that rushed over a natural stair placement of widely spaced flat rocks, then ran off a stone shelf, where it cascaded into a two-foot-high waterfall and meandered out of sight. Huge flat boulders, perfect for sitting, bordered each side of the mini-fall and sat several inches above it.

"Oh, isn't this pretty?" she softly enthused, breaking away from his hold and stepping past a profusion of ferns toward the sparkling water. She looked up to the thick canopy of tree branches that intertwined, forming a lacy arch that let only large snippets of sunshine glimmer down on them. "It's like a little outdoor grotto, almost. A special place to come and pray. This place is so beautiful. Almost as nice as the area in Hocking Hills that my father took me to when I was a girl."

Antonio regarded her as she moved in a slow circle, taking it all in. Her former awkwardness had left, and a childlike wonder made her face and eyes glow with discovery. He could almost imagine the little girl she'd been, seeing her now.

"You talk as though you've never been in these woods."

"I haven't," she admitted, puzzling Antonio anew.

Why, if she'd never visited these trails, did she choose today to start? And why pick such inappropriate clothing? Marissa was smarter than that. Memory of the half-eaten, dirt-encrusted sandwich came to mind, making him suspicious.

Had she been following him? She could've been eating her lunch when she saw him leave his house. Often these past weeks he'd spotted the sun highlighting her corn silk-colored hair while she looked outside her kitchen window, but he hadn't thought anything about it. Now he wondered. *Was* she spying on him?

She turned his way, her fine brows raised. "Is anything wrong?"

"What makes you ask?"

"You're so quiet all of a sudden."

"And is quiet bad?"

"No"—she lifted her palms in a semi-shrug—"it's just not like you."

He allowed a slight smile. "Maybe I'm just trying to figure out what would make an intelligent woman hike through the woods in a dress and heels while toting a half-eaten sandwich."

"Did I break some hiking law or something?"

"No. But you could've easily tripped on this uneven ground in those shoes and hurt yourself, so it wasn't too smart. Not to mention the damage it did to that furry sweater."

She frowned and looked at the snagged gray sleeve. "Fine. I'll make a note in my journal never to wear anything but sturdy materials and sneakers when hiking. Anything else?"

"You keep a journal?"

She nodded, her eyes wary.

This time his smile was teasing. "Judging from the past weeks, I'll bet it would make a great comedy. Maybe I should try my hand at scriptwriting?"

Her lips stretched into an I-can't-believe-you-said-that grin; then she chuckled. "Yeah, and Meg Ryan can play my part. We already know who'll play yours." An impish gleam lit her eyes.

He laughed and moved toward her. "Touché. But I doubt you could get him for such a minor role."

"Do I detect a note of jealousy?"

"No."

He lifted his hand to brush a tiny speck of what looked like dried-on lettuce from the corner of her mouth. Her warm breath soothed his flesh at the little gasp she gave, and suddenly he wished he had kissed the speck away.

He stared at her lovely features a moment longer, brushing her creamy skin with his fingertips, moving them up to her temple. Slowly he leaned toward her, his gaze going to her trembling, lower lip. Her eyes were half-closed, her mouth softened; but when their breaths mingled, she stepped backward, almost falling over herself in her haste to get away from him. Her eyes had become huge green disks.

After thick seconds of empty silence, Antonio continued, "I only meant that he would be the type to play the lead. And I'm obviously not your leading man."

Their silly game of words had ended on too awkward a note, and his husky reply added emphasis to the now uneasy atmosphere.

"I should be getting home," Marissa said quietly to the black soil beneath.

"I'll show you the way out of these woods." This time he didn't offer his hand.

Together they returned to the edge of the clearing. Before she could move in the direction of her house, Antonio spoke. "Don't forget. We have a dinner date tonight."

She jerked her head upward, her gaze finally meeting his. "That's right. . . Is casual dress okay? I've had enough of dressing nice for one day."

Relieved that she didn't break their date, he grinned. "You can wear sweat pants and a sweatshirt for all I care. Just be ready to go at seven."

Faint curiosity etched her features. "Where are we going?"

"It's a secret. I'll see you at seven." Before she could change her mind, he headed home. At the porch he hesitated and looked down the street. She, too, had paused in front of her door and was staring at him. Lifting her hand in a half wave, she scurried through the door.

Marissa intrigued him. Mystified him. Stirred him. Antonio hoped the interest was mutual and that it was only shyness that made her break away before he could kiss her. He had never thought about any woman as much as he had Marissa. And he suspected this was only the beginning.

❧

Marissa was glad she hadn't worn the suggested sweat suit.

The navy linen slacks and deep peach silk blouse fit in better with her surroundings, though she'd spotted a few of the younger diners in jeans. Antonio's navy patterned shirt and dark slacks complemented her outfit nicely, and his teasing comment when he'd first seen her—"you clean up nicely"—had made her grin.

She sat across from Antonio at a table by the window, in a new Italian restaurant she had wanted to try since she'd first heard about it. She was listening to him recount a story from his childhood in Los Angeles. So far she'd learned that most of his family lived in Spain, his uncle was a bullfighter, and his paternal grandfather was "the highly respected Don Pedro." But about Antonio himself she'd learned little. Marissa absently twined tomato and basil-covered strands of spaghetti on her fork, staring at them instead of at the disturbingly attractive man across from her.

"What made you decide to come to America?" she asked.

"I was born here."

"Oh. Do your parents live in Ohio?"

"No."

When he didn't continue, she looked up. His brown eyes seemed sad. "My mother died years ago; my father left her years before that. I stayed with an aunt. When she married and left California, I decided to pursue what little acting career I possessed. At that time I was old enough to make my own decisions."

Marissa brought the fork with spaghetti to her mouth, looked at it, and hastily lowered it to her plate in embarrassment. She cut away the huge egg-sized glob she'd twined to a more easy-to-consume portion and took a quick bite, hoping Antonio hadn't noticed. She chanced a look.

His eyes sparkled back at her. He had.

She sipped her tea and cleared her throat. "So what did bring you to Wadleyville, if it wasn't your parents?"

"Oh, this and that," he answered vaguely. "But enough about me. I want to know about you. Were you aware that Marissa is a Spanish name?"

"Yes. My great-grandmother was Spanish. I was named for her."

"Ah. And what else can you tell me about Marissa Hughes?"

She picked up her slice of garlic toast and tore a small piece away, slipping it into her mouth, choosing carefully what she would say. "Well, you know that I own and manage the bridal and floral shop, of course."

"Yes. How did that come about? Of those I know who own stores, they are in their thirties or middle-aged. You look as if you could still be in college."

"Thanks. I'm twenty-five. My father helped me get started by co-signing on a loan and offering me the rest of the money I needed to add to the nest egg I'd saved since high school. Granny left me her house in her will since Mother was her only child and I'm the only grandchild. She also left me her antiques."

Marissa worked to keep her voice steady as she slipped the bait onto the hook. "Among them are pieces of her mother's jewelry. I never had them appraised, but I suspect they're worth a small fortune. Her mother was married to a wealthy Texas rancher. When she died two years after he did, the jewelry and antiques were divided among their five children. My grandmother left what she inherited to me."

To Marissa's frustration, a dark-haired waitress with too much makeup and a roving eye for Antonio approached their table for what must have been the tenth time since they'd arrived a few minutes earlier. "Can I get you anything else?" the girl asked him sweetly.

"I'm fine." He lifted his brow Marissa's way. "Do you need anything?"

"I'd like some more tea." Marissa held out her glass and watched the waitress pour, without looking at her once. In fact, she wondered how the girl could pour the liquid and set it in front of her plate, all the while casting admiring glances at Antonio.

If Marissa weren't here solely as part of her mission to trap the man, she might be more than mildly annoyed at the young woman's avid interest in her date. Memory of the kiss they'd almost shared in the woods scattered her thoughts, and she took a swift drink of the tea to cool the warmth that rose up. She had wanted that kiss, had felt her body tingle when his breath had drifted near her lips. She set her glass down quickly. What was wrong with her? Was she getting in over her head?

"Anything wrong?" Antonio asked once the waitress had left.

Marissa's head snapped up. "What could be wrong?"

"You were glaring at that bread basket as if you would like to chuck it out the window."

She released a little breath. "Is it always like this?"

He looked at the baked bread. "It is a little black on the edges, isn't it?"

"No! Not the toast. The girl. I wonder if her other customers get asked if they want more than six refills of tea in as many minutes."

He had the audacity to grin. "Do I detect a note of jealousy?"

"Of course not," Marissa muttered, recognizing the same words she'd thrown at him earlier in the woods. "I mean, I hardly know you." She hesitated, realizing she was acting exactly the way he described. She made herself relax, even managing a smile. "I was just wondering if the girls always fawn over you, like that waitress was doing. That's all."

"I really didn't notice her. I was watching you."

His soft remark and melting eyes almost made her turn into a puddle of mush on the chair. She had to get a grip. Though, when she thought about it, he was being truthful. The entire time they'd been together his attention hadn't roved, as Grant's had always done.

The conversation was getting way too personal. Seeking neutral ground, Marissa changed the subject to a question regarding the play. The rest of the dinner was spent talking about inconsequential things. Tips on home restoration. The latest news. Marissa considered bringing up the accounts she'd read of the cat burglaries but decided not to risk it. She didn't want to scare Antonio away. Throughout the dinner, whenever she tried to bring the conversation back to him, he would offer a vague, impersonal reply in return. So when he walked her to her door later, she decided to invite him inside for coffee. Maybe, if Antonio weren't in a public environment, he would be more forthcoming about his life and less evasive with his answers.

Marissa made the coffee while Antonio sat at her pine kitchen table and watched. He wasn't big or tall, compared to some of the men she'd met, but right now he seemed to fill her little kitchen. Nervously she measured the coffee into cups and poured the boiling water from her ceramic teapot. Hot steam engulfed her hand, and she set the pot down with a bang. "Oh!"

"Did you burn yourself?" Instantly Antonio was by her side. "Let me see." He took her wrist in a gentle hold. "It's not serious. Go run it under cold water. I'll finish up."

The slight burning sensation on the back of her hand had faded, but the warmth where Antonio's palm and fingers curled around her wrist intensified. She pulled out of his light grasp and headed for the sink, dousing her hands and arms with cold water. She heard him behind her, fixing the coffee. "Do you take sugar?"

She nodded. "One spoonful. Cream, too."

As she dried off her skin, the dull clunks of saucers hitting the table caused her to turn around.

He smiled. The settings were too cozy, the chairs too close. They needed a distraction.

"I'll be back in a minute." She hurried from the kitchen and upstairs to her bedroom. Soon she returned with a long, leather-covered box and set it in the middle of the table.

Antonio was seated in one of the chairs, drinking his coffee. He lowered his cup, curiosity rampant on his face. Marissa flipped the latches of the box and opened the lid. Against a bed of black velvet, a shimmering pool of jewels was displayed—and the bait was thrown out onto the water.

Rubies inside glowed a passionate red, and deep blue sapphires gleamed almost as richly as the look in Antonio's sienna-colored eyes. A double string of diamonds winked up at them with crystal fire, coaxed into life by the overhead lights.

"May I?" he asked.

Marissa nodded and watched the fish test the bait. Antonio let out a low whistle as he picked up the diamond choker and rubbed his thumb along the gems. He laid the costly piece back on its velvet nest to pluck up a dangling sapphire earring and hold it against the light.

"Your great-grandmother had good taste," he mused. "These are high quality pieces." He peered more closely at the earring then picked up its matching necklace. "The filigree of this setting is remarkable. If you look closely, each stone is set in a gold flower, different from the last, and they're all molded as part of the necklace itself, and not separate pieces. And those diamonds are mine cut—a soft square cut that was popular in the mid-nineteenth century."

"You sound as if you know your jewelry."

"Hmm? Oh, I have a friend in California whose father is a jeweler. Remember when I said I knew some business owners? He's one of them. I got a part-time job at his store one summer." His remarks were delivered in an offhand manner.

He replaced the sapphire necklace and picked up the ruby on its slim gold chain. Cupping the large square gem in his palm, he tilted it back and forth to cause a lighter rose-colored ray within the jewel's blood-red depths to move across the smooth stone. Next he lifted a rope of pearls with a diamond clasp, feeding the necklace into his other palm and watching as the luminescent white drops pooled atop one another, into a shimmering heap of beads.

When he fingered the last piece, a ruby ring that matched the set, and laid all the jewelry back into place, he again focused his attention on Marissa. "Why don't you keep all that in a safe deposit box at the bank? It seems a little dangerous to have them lying around your home."

"Oh, I don't just keep them lying around," she explained. "There's a small safe in my bedroom. Granny got it shortly after she inherited the pieces." She hesitated. "Unless Wadleyville has a safecracker in its midst, my pieces are secure."

"Do you ever wear them?"

"Rarely. There aren't a lot of places to wear jewelry like that. I wear the pearls sometimes at the weddings I coordinate, and the ruby ring and necklace, but that's about it."

"Well, I guess you know what you're doing, but I wouldn't tell a lot of people about these." His gaze went to the jewelry again, his expression thoughtful; then he looked at his watch. "Ten forty-one. I hadn't realized it was so late. I need to call it a night." He rose from his chair and smiled. "Thanks for the coffee."

"Sure," Marissa said, a little off balance by his sudden desire to leave. "Thank you for the dinner."

She walked him to the door and opened it. He hesitated. "I had a really good time, Marissa. It was nice getting to know you a little better."

She smiled softly. "I had a good time, too." It was the truth. Often she'd had to remind herself that she was gathering evidence against this man and wasn't there to enjoy his company.

"Earlier, in the woods, I tried to kiss you without asking if it's what you wanted," he said, his voice low. "With your permission I'd like to try again."

He must have sensed her mental retreat for he quickly added, "Just a simple kiss. A thank-you-for-the-lovely-evening type of kiss."

Marissa considered the request. One simple peck at the doorstep shouldn't hurt anything. She often gave the same to the lanky, immature boys she'd dated in high school on their first dates, and some of those boys she'd never seen again. "Okay."

They smiled at each other in gentle amusement. He settled his hands at her waist. She loosely laid her palms on his shoulders, as she'd done with her high school dates. Antonio bent forward, and his warm lips touched the corner of her mouth.

Her heart leapt at the contact. Her fingers tightened and clutched hard muscle. Her nails lightly dug into his shirt.

"Marissa?" he whispered in confusion, his minty-breath soft against her cheek.

Suddenly everything changed though nothing changed. She couldn't think, couldn't answer. All she could do—all she wanted—was to close her eyes and turn her head the fraction needed for her parted lips to meet his.

His inhaled breath was quiet, short. His arms slipped more securely about her waist, bringing her closer. When his mouth brushed over hers, Marissa looped her hands around the back of his neck, tilting her mouth over his ever so slightly, encouraging him to really kiss her. He did.

Dizzying warmth swelled over Marissa, threatening to immerse her into some nearby blaze. Seconds passed before the irrationality of her behavior struck her full-force. She tore her lips away from his, removing her fingers from his hair, where they'd somehow become entwined in the silken, dark locks. Stunned, she leaned back, and Antonio let her go.

Marissa took a hasty step in retreat, partially stumbling over the stoop, and found safety inside the house, beside the open door, which she clutched like the barrier it was. His dark gaze threatened to consume her, but he didn't move a muscle.

"I–I didn't mean for that to happen." Her voice was hoarse. "It's—it's been a long time since—I'm sorry."

"No apology necessary." His voice sounded strained. "Good night, Marissa."

"Good night." She shut the door with a faint click and leaned against it, putting her fingers to her lips still warm from his kisses.

What was wrong with her? And who was she kidding? It had been a long time since she'd been kissed, yes, but when Grant kissed her, he'd never elicited the response Antonio had. Grant had been something like her house cat, offering affection when it suited him, cuddling up to her when he desired it, but fickle, often wandering away. And she didn't find out about his late-night strolls with other women until after the fact. She once thought of Grant as warm, comfortable, and loyal—before she'd discovered he was a philandering tomcat in disguise.

But Antonio. . .Antonio possessed the nature of a wildcat. Passionate. Dangerous. Able to cause a girl's heart to beat triple-time then melt with one mere look from his gypsy-dark eyes, one kiss from his sensitive lips.

Groaning at her sheer stupidity, Marissa headed for the kitchen, collected her jewels, and went upstairs to return them to the safe. Such outbursts of emotion could never be allowed to resurface. Tonight would serve as a warning to her, not to step over the hidden line she'd drawn between them. The fault had been entirely her own. She'd been the one to cross that line, to reach out for more, almost begging him to give it. Yet with Antonio, she realized, there could be no such thing as a "simple kiss." Not for her. He was most likely a thief.

And she was falling hard for him.

Marissa slammed the safe door closed and twirled the knob. Shutting her eyes, she fell back to sit against the papered wall. How could she even consider liking a man who played games with the law and mocked the police with his yellow roses? She was definitely in over her head. But it was too late to back out now.

The trap was set.

seven

Just as Antonio opened the door of the ice cream shop, he spotted Marissa peering around the rose-brick building rimmed in fluorescent white light. He closed the door and looked to the corner, where he knew he'd seen her image through the glass.

"Marissa?"

A few seconds elapsed before she stepped onto the brightly lit sidewalk. "Hi." She gave a nervous, jerky little wave, barely moving her hand from her purse strap.

"What brings you here? I thought you had to get home after play practice."

"Um, actually I had to run some errands. I thought I'd stop in for a quick bite to eat."

"Yeah," Antonio said slowly, his mind going a mile a minute. "Same here."

Had she been following him again? If so, he considered that very strange since she'd shown little interest in him tonight—barely making eye contact with him during play practice, then disappearing from church almost before Mike could finish announcing that practice was over.

Antonio opened the door again, allowing her to go in ahead of him. "I hate to eat alone," he said. "Care to join me?"

She nodded and moved past him. They stared up at the backlit menu. The syrupy sweet smell of maraschino cherries lingered in the air, and Antonio saw a gray-haired man sopping up red juice from a spill on the counter. A small "Help Wanted" sign sat near the register.

"What's your favorite flavor?" Antonio asked Marissa.

"I don't care for ice cream. That is"—two faint lines appeared between her eyebrows—"I think I'd rather just have a cup of hot chocolate. I'm not that hungry."

Didn't she just say she was hungry? The menu advertised only ice cream desserts, so if she'd come here for a "quick bite" what was she planning on biting?

The elderly man waited on them, and Marissa insisted she buy her beverage. She gave two dollars to the man before Antonio could argue; then they headed to a far booth. Antonio licked a stream of chocolate that seeped from his rocky-road double mound and made a trail down the napkin-wrapped sugar cone.

He slid into the orange booth across from Marissa and regarded her soberly. "Actually I'm glad you decided to come here tonight. I've wanted to call you, but I don't have your number. And I didn't want to show up at your front door uninvited."

She took a sip of hot chocolate topped with whipped cream then set it down fast and blotted the white foam from her upper lip. Her eyes were grave. "Antonio, before you go any further, I need to tell you something. I don't want to get involved in a serious relationship—with anyone. What happened Sunday night"—a light flush colored her face—"that was a mistake, and I'm sorry."

Antonio had thought a lot about that kiss. When he first met Marissa in her shop, he'd classified her as a cool blond. But the woman who'd kissed him Saturday night exhibited a taste of buried passion he hoped one day he might have the right to explore fully. Of course, he knew that meant marriage, and if he were financially stable he would pursue Marissa. He felt a strong connection to her that he'd felt for no other woman, more than just a physical pull. Her desire for old-fashioned things and her moral character reminded him of his grandmother. That she possessed Spanish ancestry would win points of favor from his family as well.

Still, there was so much about Marissa that remained a mystery. Her eyes, like the tiger lily, softly entreated, "I dare you to love me," even while her lips told him she wanted only his friendship. To make Marissa fall in love with him wouldn't be difficult, Antonio surmised, but he didn't want to push anyone into doing something the person wasn't freely willing to do. Then, too, he wouldn't be satisfied with anything less than the total affection they could share. Which again led him back to marriage.

She was right. Her idea was the safest road to take—for now.

"Okay. Just friends it is." He took a large bite of ice cream, chilling his teeth.

Unguarded disappointment shone in her eyes before she lowered her gaze to her cup. "Good." She blew on the hot chocolate to cool it then took a smaller sip. "Now that we have that behind us, I'd like to discuss the play. I can't believe it's in less than two weeks."

They spent the next ten minutes talking about small problems that needed correcting and how to go about them. Antonio sensed that she still didn't want to be in the play, but she didn't balk as before. Soon the conversation eased into the topic of her business.

Antonio crunched into the last of the cone he'd been holding for the past few minutes as he sat, enraptured by her enthusiasm, while she discussed her plans for a wedding chapel.

"I admire you, Marissa. Not everyone grabs hold of their goals and pursues their dreams as you've done."

Her oval, peach-colored nails traced the sides of her cup. "Do you have a dream?"

"Everyone has a dream." He released a one-note, self-mocking laugh. "But not everyone has the ability to see that dream become reality."

"Oh, I don't believe that." She reached out to lay her hand lightly over his on the table, surprising him. Her eyes were intent as she leaned forward. "God gives everyone a dream, Antonio. He makes His desires our own when we fully give Him our lives. I'm not just talking about saying a one-time prayer, either—I'm talking about making Him a part of your life every day. Then, and only then, will He give you your heart's desires. Because as you grow closer to Him, His desires become yours. The desire to please Him becomes paramount, and at the same time you experience your dreams—the dreams He imbedded in you from the start."

Suddenly she pulled her hand away, as if just realizing she'd touched him. "Wow!" She gave a light chuckle. "Where'd that come from? I didn't mean to go on so."

"No." He leaned forward slightly. "I'm glad you brought it up. But sometimes the direction to go gets hazy, life interferes, and it's easy to get off course. What then?"

"At times like that, you just have to hold on to God more tightly and trust Him to get you through the hard times." Her expression was somber. "I learned that the hard way. First through my mother's death, then through Grant's betrayal. Relying on God for my business ventures was a cake walk after that."

"Grant?"

She stiffened. "My ex-fiancé of a year ago. To say I got burned seems trivial. More like annihilated." Looking down at the table, she shrugged. "Grant didn't believe in monogamous relationships, a fact I was grateful to discover before the wedding could take place."

"Then Grant was an idiot."

"That's what his mom said." She gave a half smile. "But let's not talk about him. I'd like to hear what your long-range goals and dreams are, if you don't mind telling them to me—friend to friend."

Looking at her, he wished he could take her in his arms and soothe all her hurts away. He detected a trace of pain still lingering behind her lovely green eyes.

"One day, Marissa, I hope to do just that." *And as much more than a friend,* he added silently.

❧

Marissa blew into her steaming cup of coffee as she hurried down the sunny sidewalk, almost running into a man who suddenly blocked her way.

"Marissa? What are you doing out of the shop? Did you take the day off?"

"Hi—I just took the afternoon off, not the whole day." She shaded her eyes with one hand and smiled up at Antonio. He looked wonderful in a snowy white sport shirt and dark jeans, with his hair pulled back in a short ponytail. It was the first she'd ever seen him wear a light color—the first she'd seen him in over a week, except for at play practice. Last Saturday she had waited up late, to try to catch him breaking into her house for the jewels, but he never did. And there were no reported thefts anywhere else that night either. If he were the cat burglar, she hoped this meant he'd decided to give up the profession.

"The new employees are working out great," Marissa said. "Gladys is proving she's earned the title of assistant, and, wonder of wonders, the computer my dad gave me is actually proving to be a time-saver rather than the thorn in my side I'd thought it would be. Maybe I shouldn't play hooky today, with the spring season in full swing, not to mention the huge influx of Easter orders, but I thought I'd take a few hours away from the shop for a breather."

He grinned. "You sound as if you're in a good mood. Where are you off to?"

"An auction. I haven't been to one in awhile. You?".

"I'm out looking for a birthday gift."

Marissa thought a moment. She didn't want to admit it, but she had missed his company. Besides, she should dig deeper into the file of Antonio Ramirez—and she'd like to know whom the birthday gift was for. A relative? Or a girlfriend?

"Would you like to come with me to the auction?" she asked. "Some of the starting bids are steep, but you might find something."

He looked uncertain. "What kind of auction is it?"

"Art. Furniture. Some books. All antiques."

"I see you're wearing the jewelry."

She glanced at the ruby ring on her finger. "It seemed like the right thing to wear to an antique auction, and this outfit needed something."

He eyed her satiny black blouse appreciatively. Or was it the ruby necklace he admired?

"It looks great on you," he murmured then lifted his gaze to hers. "Sure. I'll come and check it out. Can I catch a ride?"

"Okay." They'd reached a mutual agreement that a serious relationship was out of the question and friendship was all they would share. So why did Marissa's heart skip a few crazy beats at the prospect of having Antonio with her for the next few hours? She inhaled deeply as she slid behind her wheel and waited for him to buckle his seatbelt.

Be still, you foolish heart.

"Ready when you are." He sent Marissa a smile that challenged her pulse to remain steady. Did the man have to be so undeniably attractive?

Looking away, she put the car in gear and drove to the outskirts of town and the new single-story ranch-style building at the edge of the woods where the auction was being held. The Ripleys, a well-traveled couple who had planted their roots in Wadleyville three years ago, made a habit of frequenting estate sales and other treasure troves for the items they sold. Marissa had visited their auctions twice last year and looked forward to seeing what items would be offered today. She'd come early, since she hadn't been able to view the antiques open to public display the past week.

Inside the building the Ripleys' daughter greeted them, her smile seeming extra bright for Antonio. Telling herself she wasn't jealous, Marissa focused her attention on the room where the auction was usually held. The doors were closed instead of wide open to the public.

"We had a little accident in there—a child got sick," the redhead explained, directing them toward a corridor that led to the back of the house. "This close to auction time, Mother decided it best to move the proceedings outside since it's not cold or rainy today."

"Will I still get to view the items ahead of time?" Marissa asked.

"Of course. Many of them are displayed on tables outside, at the back."

They were shown to a grassy clearing sprinkled with wildflowers. Marissa spotted clusters of blue phlox, whose petals resembled miniature fan blades, as well as the rose-pink blooms of another type of flower, whose five-pointed petals bent upward resembling the shooting stars for which they were named. Trees towered on three sides. A green and white striped awning stood over rows of cushion-seated folding chairs divided into two sections. At the front a podium stood, and on each side of it tables held the wares to be auctioned.

Many seats were already filled, but Marissa saw only the dainty pair of twentieth-century table lamps that winked at her from the end of a table. She made a beeline for them. Delicate, tear-dropped crystal prisms caught the light from the lavender-draped shade, and the base was of ornate silver. One would blend perfectly in her bedroom; the other would work well as decor for the round guest-book table at weddings.

She shot a glance at the rest of the items on the tables and at the bigger furniture on the covered wooden patio, but her mind was already made up. She wanted the lamps.

"Find anything?" She moved next to Antonio.

He touched a white fluted vase of French design that bore painted yellow roses and butterflies with touches in gold leaf. "This is nice. How much do you think it will go for?"

Of course. He would choose something connected with yellow roses.

Marissa eyed the piece, noting its quality. "I would think the starting bid on that would be somewhere around fifty dollars. But, of course, I'm no expert."

"Fifty dollars?" He slowly withdrew his hand from the rim, as though his touch might suddenly crack it.

"I've seen similar vases go for as much as two hundred dollars."

"It looks as if they're about to start." His gaze went to the sea of brown chairs. "Let's go find a seat."

Marissa retrieved a bidding card with a number from the girl who'd greeted them, then took a place beside Antonio, who sat on the outside seat in the back row. "You need to go get one of these if you want to bid. You give them your name, and they give you a number."

"People don't call their bids out? That's the way I've seen it done in the movies."

She smiled. "I've been to those kinds of auctions, too. Each auction is different, I've come to find out. Those in charge pick the methods that suit them best. You'd better hurry if •

you want to get a number, though. Once the auction starts, it's too late."

He considered a moment. "I don't think I'll join in this time."

"Then I'm sorry you wasted an afternoon. I should've realized this would be too pricey for you, especially since you don't have a job right now—" She broke off, realizing she had inadvertently revealed that she'd been keeping daily track of his whereabouts.

He looked at her sharply, and she offered him a dumb-me-little-smile while flapping a tiny bug away from her face. "I mean, I'm guessing you don't have a job since I never see you leave on weekday mornings, and your car is usually in the drive when I get home." Oh, terrific. That sounded even worse. As if she were keeping a daily journal of his movements, which in a way she was, but she didn't want him to know it.

He studied her a moment before replying. "You're right. I don't have a steady, nine-to-five job, and this probably isn't the best place for me to buy a gift right now, but I don't consider my afternoon wasted. I enjoy being with you, Marissa."

She wished his admission didn't make her feel so good inside. Uncomfortable, she focused her attention on a tall man who took his place behind the podium. At the ice cream shop Antonio agreed to being just friends—much more quickly than Marissa would have believed—and she wouldn't allow herself to nurture any feelings other than friendly ones. After all, she didn't want anything more and had told him so.

Marissa settled back and watched the proceedings. When the auctioneer only brought one of the lamps forward, she was disappointed to see that they weren't auctioning off the pair as a set and wondered why. She bid against another woman in a broad black hat, sitting on the front row, and quit at $375. Marissa was disappointed, but she'd promised herself not to exceed $400. When the next lamp was brought up, she sat forward in her chair, hearing Antonio's chuckled murmur of, "Go for it, Tiger."

She ignored him, again bidding against the woman in the hat, who thankfully didn't up Marissa's winning bid of $325.

Marissa settled back with a triumphant smile. She couldn't help, though, hearing the woman in the row in front of her whisper loudly to her companion, "I saw a similar set go for $450 for the pair a month ago. Looks like they made a profit in selling them separately."

The woman's observation didn't dampen Marissa's joy. She would take her new lamp from home, as needed, to any wedding that matched the scheme. She did that with other personal items sometimes, too. It was all insured.

Something flew into her eye, making it sting and water. She pushed her bidding card toward Antonio, with a muffled "hold this, please," and grabbed her purse from the ground. Fumbling her compact open, she stared into the round mirror and pulled the skin down under her eye, hoping it wasn't an insect she was searching for. The rain last night had brought them back with a vengeance, and the clouds in the north were tinged gray now, forecasting more rain ahead.

The bidding continued, and she heard the auctioneer's amused voice. "Sir, you can't outbid yourself."

People chuckled, and Marissa lifted her head to see, one eye squinted shut. She groaned audibly and grabbed Antonio's wrist, to stop him from flapping the bidding card. "What're you doing?" she whispered.

"It's these bugs," he muttered, using his other hand to swat at a tiny, pesky black insect flying near his face.

"Antonio," she wailed softly, "you just bid on that item using my card!"

"What?" He looked to the front then at her. "How can that be? I didn't raise it up in the air like the others are doing."

"It doesn't matter. With the way you were swatting it, it looked as if you were bidding." She rubbed her index finger beneath her eye and blinked rapidly, trying to get rid of whatever was in it. Sensing his unease, she muttered, "Don't worry. Maybe someone will outbid you. Just don't move a muscle!"

But her worst fears were realized with the auctioneer's next words: "Sold, to the gentleman in the back row for nine hundred and fifty dollars."

Marissa groaned. "Congratulations," she whispered to Antonio. "You've just become the proud owner of a 1910 curio cabinet."

❧

"Almost a thousand dollars?" Antonio was sure he was going to be sick.

"I've seen them go for twice that," Marissa said. "Obviously no one else was serious about buying curio cabinets today."

The comment did little to make Antonio feel better. "Can't we just tell them it was all an honest mistake?" he whispered, using his hands in a half shrug as bidding began for another item.

Marissa slowly but forcefully slid the stick holding the numbered card from his hand then wiped the dampness from underneath her one watery eye. "It doesn't work that way, but never mind. I have a curio cabinet at home, but I suppose I could always put one in the shop, to use as a display. I don't expect you to pay for it. I know it's more than you can afford."

Her sympathetic comment ruffled his pride. He wasn't a destitute bum, which is how she made him sound. The purchase, along with the repairs his car needed, would take a huge chunk of his diminishing savings, and he would need to look for a day job sooner than he'd thought, one that didn't conflict with his weekends. Yet the last thing he was going to do was let Marissa pay for his mistake.

"No," he said pulling his checkbook from his back jeans pocket. "This isn't your problem. It's mine."

She put her hand over the one holding his checkbook open. "Please, Antonio. I don't mind."

He looked at her, sensing her slight distress over his situation. "It won't make me a pauper, Marissa. I appreciate the offer—and it *is* a little more than I intended to pay—but it'll make a nice gift." Actually it was a lot more than he'd intended to pay for the birthday present. A whole lot more. He might have to live on canned tuna and peanut butter and crackers for awhile, and it would mean no more dinner dates with Marissa, something he'd planned to continue, despite their friends-only status, but he'd manage. Maybe he could find a buyer soon. He would do whatever he had to, within reason, to bring in more income.

The light in Marissa's eyes seemed to go out, and he visibly detected her withdrawal. "Oh, well, if you insist. But you aren't supposed to pay for it until after the auction's ended."

Antonio slipped his checkbook back in his pocket and sat beside a mute Marissa until the end of the auction. He was puzzled at why she should seem so offended by his refusal for her to pay for an item she obviously didn't want or need. Afterward, when they made their payments, Marissa coolly mentioned that the glass and wood cabinet probably wouldn't fit into her car without possibly causing the item damage. Antonio grudgingly added an extra twenty-five dollars to the total for the four-foot high cabinet to be delivered, giving the auction hostess the address where it was to go. Arrangements made, he turned to look at Marissa.

A redheaded woman in a black hat stood beside her, admiring Marissa's ruby necklace, and Antonio recognized her as the lady who'd won the other lamp. Next to her stood a bored-looking young man of slight build. The woman kept directing comments his way, as if hoping to bring the blond man into their conversation, but he didn't speak. He wore an onyx cross in one ear. The woman also wore jewels over the blouse of her black pantsuit—a crescent moon-shaped silver necklace with pear-shaped jet stones surrounded by sprays of tiny diamonds.

Antonio could almost hear his former employer's voice in his head. "A nice piece—fits her personality. But much too ostentatious to wear during daylight hours." The old jeweler always did have an eye for matching specific pieces to a person's character. Mr. Rosenthal had taught Antonio much of what he knew, including how to tell the genuine article from a fake, but he never was able to pass on to Antonio his knack for matching jewelry with people. Much like Marissa matched flowers to the proper occasion.

He studied Marissa, looking so classic and smart, yet ultra-feminine, too. As though sensing his stare, she glanced away from the woman and met his gaze. For a moment her expression was unguarded, and Antonio saw a soft yearning that made him widen his eyes. She quickly averted her gaze, addressing a question to the man—one he'd just answered.

Antonio watched Marissa grow suddenly talkative, too much so, a sure sign she was upset. In spending time with her these past weeks, especially during play practices, he had learned to read what she was feeling. And for the second time in just over a week, he wished he hadn't agreed that they remain just friends.

The drive to their neighborhood was quiet, save for the crystal teardrops tinkling from the lampshade, whose base was securely nestled in towels against the back seat. Once Marissa pulled into her driveway, Antonio muttered his thanks and opened the door to swing one foot to the gravel. But before he could fully exit the car, Marissa spoke.

"I guess I'll see you at dress rehearsal Saturday? Mike said to be there at three. Oh, that's right. You weren't at church Sunday when the announcement was made, but surely you heard about it last night at practice—right?"

"Yes, I heard. But I'm not sure I can make it. I told Mike that if I could come for an hour, I would, but I can't make any promises."

Marissa frowned. "Mike's depending on you to be there, Antonio. You're the director. You have to be there. I'll be late—I need to get the Easter orders ready for delivery—but I'm going. He plans to let us out around seven. They're having pizza delivered so no one will starve."

"As I said, if I can possibly make it for an hour or so, I will."

Question marks danced in Marissa's eyes. "Maybe you could put off your other business for just one week?" The question came out tart, almost accusing. "Surely that's not a lot to ask?"

"Maybe," he agreed tightly, sending her a faint smile before climbing out of the car.

Walking back to his house, he pondered his dilemma. He couldn't let Mike and the kids down. But he couldn't disappoint the other people who depended on him either. Yet how was he supposed to be in two places at once? Much as he hated to do it, he would have to call and change his plans to a different day or skip this week altogether. He hoped that wouldn't present a problem.

Thinking about Marissa's comment of his missing church, Antonio experienced a twinge of guilt pricking his conscience. A sinus headache had been the excuse for his absence the first Sunday, when he'd run across Marissa in the woods, and his car hadn't started this past Sunday. But if he were honest with himself, he would have to admit he hadn't wanted to be there.

He'd made a mess of his life in L.A., hanging out with people he shouldn't have. He had slipped, bit by bit, further from the faith his grandmother instilled in him as a child during her and Grandfather's summer visits to California. He'd made his peace with the Lord when he hit his twenties. But somehow he'd forgotten his good intentions to live a decent life these past few years and had become more and more like his actor friends. Greedy. Selfish. Doing things he shouldn't do.

The letter from his grandmother drew him out of Hollywood's cesspool, and Antonio was now glad for that, but it was difficult to sit in church without feeling like a complete failure. As if he shouldn't even be there. After hearing miraculous testimonies about God working in other people's lives, he wondered if he fit in. Sometimes, like today, he wished he hadn't jumped to volunteer with the Easter play, despite his love for drama. He'd never intended to speak up, but some strong force within had compelled him forward, like a bullfighter enticing a bull in the ring. He knew sometimes he could be as ornery as one of the snorting beasts, or so his mother once said—like his father, who had left his wife of five years and small son and cleared out their bank account. His mother had to turn to her family for financial aid, though she'd insisted on staying in California, sure her son could make it there as a child star. That had been a joke. The few spots he'd gotten in commercials and bit parts in movies hadn't done much to help in those days. His mother had still needed to get a job as a waitress, and Antonio was left with his free-thinking, single aunt a lot of the time.

Maybe if Antonio's father had never left, his mother wouldn't have been so persistent with Antonio's seemingly endless acting lessons and screen tests. Then he could have enjoyed a normal childhood as other kids had. Maybe if he hadn't seen his mother scrape and scrounge until her death, he wouldn't be so concerned about making a lot of money. And maybe, if he'd had a father to raise him, he could get a right perspective on life.

He let himself into his house. No. It did no good to blame his past and what he was or wasn't. It was up to him to make a difference. He thought of what Marissa had said about following one's dreams and how people could realize their dreams only by giving their desires to God, fully submitting their lives to Him. Maybe it was the only way.

Antonio just wasn't sure he was ready for it.

eight

Crossing her arms over her chest, Marissa leaned her veiled head and shoulder against the dark corridor wall on the other side of the sanctuary and let the tears that had sprung up out of nowhere silently flow. A widening rectangle of golden light alerted her to the fact that someone had opened the door behind her. She straightened with a little sniffle, hoping the intruder couldn't tell she'd been crying.

"Miss Hughes?" Genna's uncertain voice came from behind her. "Is everything okay?"

Marissa ran the backs of her fingers under her eyes and turned to face the child with a bright smile, one that faltered upon seeing Antonio standing in back of the girl. His expression under the brown cotton turban was a mask of concern.

"You did really well," Genna said. "I would've been scared if you hadn't been standing by me when I had to say those lines. So please don't feel bad, Miss Hughes. Anyone could've tripped on their robe if they'd been wearing one as long as yours. At least you didn't fall on Chris—you just bumped him a little. And he probably stepped on his own big foot."

Antonio set his hands atop Genna's shoulders. "Genna, why don't you go ask the other kids to put their costumes and props back in the boxes before they go home? With all the excitement of rushing to egg hunts and Easter baskets, they might forget."

She smiled as she craned her head to look back at him. "I got a huge white chocolate bunny with crushed Oreos in it.

But Mama says I have to eat all my ham and green beans and corn before I get any."

"Well, you know what they say, Genna. Mama knows best." Marissa tried to make her words sound light, but they came out strained instead.

"I thought that was 'Father knows best,'" Antonio inserted with a smile.

"It's just not fair," Genna said. "Chris ate all his candy before church this morning. . . 'Course, Mama and Daddy don't know. 'Bye!" A mischievous twinkle of a sister about to tell on her brother entered Genna's eyes before she scampered away, the hem of her blue cloak she'd worn as Mary flapping behind her.

"Hank and Jenny certainly have their hands full," Marissa told Antonio, feeling a little self-conscious with the way he was staring at her. "Did you see Hank? He was in clown gear today for the little tots' church. You couldn't miss him. He was the one with the Afro colored like an Easter egg." To her horror her voice cracked, and she felt another onslaught of tears prick her eyes. The bridge of her nose stung with the pressure.

Wordlessly, Antonio took hold of her elbow and moved with her down the dark hall toward the glowing red exit sign. He pushed on the door's silver cross bar with a metallic *thunk* and led her outside.

Through tear-blurred vision, Marissa saw that the back parking lot held only three cars. Most everyone had departed, probably anxious to consume bountiful feasts of Easter dinners. If Marissa had taken the time to shop, she would have made a special meal for her and her dad, too. But the recent onslaught of weddings, plus all the floral Easter orders, had taken everything she had in her. A chill wind bit through her heel-length brown canvas tunic and the dress she wore underneath, and she crossed her arms again. Her calendar might say spring had arrived, but it didn't feel like it.

"Want to tell me what's upsetting you?" Antonio queried softly. "Is this about your little misstep?"

She shook her head no, hesitated, then moved the few inches toward him and laid her right temple against his chest. He felt so warm and stable. Tears wet her cheeks again.

Instantly he slipped his arms around the middle of her back, soothing, reassuring, a silent witness to testify that he was there for her. They stood that way a long time, with him swaying slightly from side to side, rocking her, while the wind blew their headdresses in their faces and their long tunics flapped about their legs.

When she felt she could talk and the emotional episode had ended, Marissa pulled away, rubbing the wetness from her cheeks with her fingertips. She noted his brown headdress and the noose, which still hung from the back of his neck, over his dark red tunic. She tried to grin. "You know, you look good in that costume. You played the part of Judas well."

"I'll take that as a compliment," he said, though the expression in his eyes was one of gentle probing. "It's too bad Randy missed out, though. I probably looked like a giant standing amid a bunch of midget apostles."

Marissa hadn't minded that fact and didn't think anyone else did either. Antonio was the only one who knew the play by heart and had gallantly stepped in when a harried Mike received the last minute phone call from Randy's mom, with news that the boy had a stomach virus and couldn't be there. Antonio had given emotion to his characterization of Judas, displaying a hint of what a great actor he was. Still, he hadn't taken over the play and had let the kids have the spotlight, even silently urging the younger ones from his place on stage, with just a look or a nod. Marissa admired him for that.

"It was a good play Sandy wrote," she said, her gaze dropping to his chest. "It touched a lot of people."

"And you?" He gently hooked his finger under her chin and lifted it, so he could see into her eyes.

She gave a slight nod. "And me."

"I can spare a few minutes if you want to talk."

For the first time in a long time, she did. "Can we get out of these costumes first? I keep thinking the wind is going to tear this headdress off and I'll have to chase it across the parking lot."

He laughed. "Sure. I'm anxious to get out of this rig myself."

Together they entered the building and headed to the children's church area, where they'd dressed. Once they pulled off the veils and tunics that covered their Sunday clothes and laid them in the box, Antonio escorted Marissa out the front door where an usher hurried to and fro, in his effort to lock up and go home.

"Let's sit in my car," Marissa said to Antonio. "This wind is really strong."

Once they were settled in the front bucket seats, she chewed on her bottom lip awhile before she looked at him. "The play and the choir's singing did touch me, but in a way I wasn't expecting."

"Oh?"

She drew her brows together, sorting out what she would say. "In the play Lorie begged God to show her proof that her older brother was in heaven and wasn't hurting anymore, and a flower budded on that dead plant Easter morning. I remembered something that happened after my mom died—something I'd forgotten over the years. At the time I was too torn up to think about it much. I was eleven then, and being an adult now I thought I'd dealt with losing her. But seeing that play in its finality brought it all back. The feelings, everything."

"The play never affected you before this?"

She shook her head. "We did it in bits and pieces, not altogether. Also, remember, I was sometimes late for practices because of weddings or business at the shop—Easter is always hectic for a florist. So I missed that part about the miracle during dress rehearsal, because I was in the back helping the younger kids change into their costumes for the finale. Today Sheila, one of the mothers, took over that job."

He nodded, and Marissa took a deep breath, willing her voice not to shake. "When Mama died, I was devastated. Even expecting her death all those months didn't help relieve the sorrow. I ran through the fields behind the house until I couldn't run anymore. As I sat on the grass, crying, with my face buried in my knees, I felt something soft tickle my finger. I lifted my head to look and saw the most beautiful jewel-toned butterfly. The light seemed to shine through its wings, making them look like stained glass. Even when I moved my hand, it stayed on my finger, its wings moving slowly up and down. It never once tried to fly away. I kept staring at it, until I felt strangely at peace—though over the years I'd forgotten about that afternoon. But it was as if God was reaching down from heaven to touch me."

"The butterfly is a sign of resurrection," Antonio said quietly, obviously moved by her story.

Marissa was surprised he would know such a thing. "Yes, but I didn't know that then. Now I see it as if the Lord was telling me, just as He told Lorie something similar in the play, 'Yes, child. Your mother is here with Me, and she's happy and without pain.' That's why I was crying. Because I felt as if something within had finally been released and was starting to heal. Something I didn't even know was trapped inside."

There was more. More she didn't want to tell Antonio. She had used her mother's death as an excuse to withdraw from the world, though the withdrawal had been a gradual one. She could see that now. As an only child she and her mother had been very close. Marissa's preference to remain in the background and live her solitary existence with her cat had been a defense mechanism to ward off the possibility of losing someone dear to her again—first her mom, then her granny. Even with her dad, she maintained a mental distance though she was quick to show him her love with a hug. Meeting Grant had been a fluke; he'd been the one to prod her into going out with him until she'd finally said yes. But Antonio. . .Antonio didn't prod or even cajole. He respected her desire to keep their relationship on a friends-only basis, and she should be relieved about the lack of pressure on his part.

So why wasn't she relieved?

"Do you have plans for Easter dinner?" Marissa asked before she could think about it. "I'm eating out with my dad, but you're welcome to join us if you'd like."

If he was surprised by her rapid-fire change of subject, he didn't show it. "Yes, I do have plans. But thanks for asking."

"Sure." She kept the companionable smile on her face though her heart did a little nosedive into the stagnant pool of disappointment. He must be having dinner with the unknown girlfriend for whom he'd bought the curio cabinet. Such an expensive gift had to be for a loved one, and he'd never mentioned any family, except those in Spain. Surely he wouldn't send such a fragile item all the way to that country?

She forced cheerfulness into her tone. "Well, thanks for listening. It helped to talk about it with someone."

"I'm honored to have been that someone." His voice was silky soft. "Anytime you want to talk, I'd be happy to be that someone again. I'm here for you, Rissa."

He stepped out of her car. His endearing use of her name and the charming smile he gave before he walked away sent her heart jumping into the clouds again. Why did he affect her so?

Driving to meet her father at the local restaurant they'd agreed upon, Marissa tried to sort through her list of mental questions. But she didn't like any of the answers she came up with.

⁂

Catching sight of the new customers who entered the almost empty shop, Antonio said under his breath to the elderly man beside him, "I'll take these two."

Hal nodded and headed toward an open area of dirty tables with a wet washcloth. Marissa and Judy stared at Antonio in surprise.

"When did you start working here?" Marissa asked.

"The week after Easter." Antonio clutched the end of the pale orange counter, his hands a few feet apart in a casual stance, and leaned slightly toward the women. "What can I get for you ladies?"

"I'll take a classic banana split, extra cherries," Judy said without missing a beat.

"And you?" he asked Marissa.

"I'm not sure yet. Give me a minute."

Antonio peeled and halved a banana then scooped up a mound each of vanilla, strawberry, and chocolate ice cream and dropped them into an oval plastic dish.

Judy leaned closer to the glass case displaying an appetizing rainbow of twenty-two round containers of ice cream flavors. "If I'd known you needed work, I would've offered you the job of driving my catering van and helping to set things up for events. It's time we found someone new."

Antonio gave her an easy smile as he spooned thick, gooey globs of hot fudge sauce over the Neapolitan ice cream globes.

"I appreciate it, Judy, but I needed a job with weekends off."
He didn't miss the sharp glance Marissa directed Judy's way.
"And most catering jobs are held on weekends, right?"

Judy nodded, the expression on her face much more
relaxed than Marissa's.

Antonio spritzed fluffy clouds of whipped cream on both
sides of the dish and atop the fudge. "This isn't so bad. I had
a job like it in high school, so it wasn't hard to learn. Actors
often run a gamut of jobs until they hope to find that one
successful script that will launch them into stardom. They
have to if they want to eat." He sprinkled chopped peanuts
on top, added six glossy cherries then set the treat atop the
glass counter display. "There," he said with a smile. "Okay?"

"Perfect," Judy murmured as though she were in heaven.
"You did that really fast, and it's a work of art. I imagine Hal
is glad he hired you."

"The feeling is mutual." He rang up her purchase, took her
money then looked at Marissa. "Since you don't like ice cream,
will you let me choose something I think you would like?"

Her green eyes widened. "I—sure. But it's not that I don't
like ice cream. It's just that I don't need all the extra calories.
Judy uses me as her one-woman tasting board for the bakery,
since her creations are used at weddings I coordinate. Not
that I mind—her pastries are out of this world—but that
means I have to watch what I eat elsewhere."

"As far as the calories go, that's debatable," he said, winking.
"A little extra on a woman is just that much more for a man to
love. But I'll honor your wish. Now will you trust me?"

She stared at him as if in a daze but nodded.

Judy gave Antonio a big grin as she picked up her dessert and
headed toward the booth. "Grab him before he gets away," she
said in a stage whisper, near Marissa's shoulder, with an amused
glance at Antonio. "This one's too good to throw back."

"Just ignore her." Marissa's face deepened to a becoming shade of rose that matched the flowers in her gray blouse. "She thinks that because she's happily married, everyone else should be, too."

"That's not a bad idea," Antonio murmured, watching her eyes widen even more. He gave her an easy grin. "Go join your friend and stop looking at me as if I may jump over the counter and gobble you up. I'll bring your dessert to your table."

He watched her for a few moments as she quickly moved to join Judy. Why were women so weight-conscious when men would eat almost anything put in front of them? Marissa was perfect, but several more pounds wouldn't hurt her either.

Antonio set about creating the customized dessert. He supposed Hollywood and the glamour girls of tinsel town were partially responsible for making women think they had to be thin sticks with curves to appeal to a man. His mother and aunt had been slightly plump, but that hadn't kept dates from knocking on their doors. He'd dated a girl once, an actress, who thought the only way to happiness was through the diet pills she consumed daily to make herself model-thin. She was still in a hospital, being treated for eating disorders, and Antonio supposed that's why he felt so strongly about the subject. Upon first meeting her, Kim had been a typical fresh, hometown girl who came to Hollywood with stars in her eyes, sure a talent scout would nab her the first day and make her a star. But what that city had made of her was far from that. The last time he'd seen Kim, she resembled a gaunt specter of her former self, with a cynical attitude to match.

Every day that passed increased Antonio's relief to be out of the glitzy, artificial world in which he'd grown up and in this small, picturesque town. Here people smiled and talked to you on the shady, tree-lined sidewalks, and parking meters cost only a nickel. His Saturday nights were beginning to pay off, too. He was doubly glad now that he'd responded to Joe's letter. And then there was Marissa. . . .

When he finished the one-of-a kind special, Antonio took it to their booth and set the tall, frosted ice cream glass in front of her. She stared into the mint-green smoothie with the red swirl, her expression uncertain, and Antonio chuckled.

"I promise it's not laced with arsenic. Try it."

Tentatively she picked up the long-handled spoon and skimmed it over the top, collecting a baby-sized portion at the tip. She slid it partially between her lips, and her eyes widened in delight. "This is delicious." She took another spoonful, this one heaping.

"Lime and pineapple sherbet with a dash of cherry syrup thrown in for good measure."

She looked a little stunned. "They're my favorites."

"I know."

"You know?" she whispered, her eyes going rounder.

He hunkered down beside her booth seat, using his hand on the table for balance, and looked up at her. "I could let you go on thinking I had a knack for picking out flavors to suit individuals, like you do flowers, but I'll confess. I saw the empty sherbet cartons on your kitchen counter that evening when I came inside to look at your jewelry."

"Really?" Judy drawled in a mockingly amused tone, her brow arching. "This sounds as if it could be interesting. She showed you her antique jewelry?"

"Please, Judy. Let's not go there." Marissa turned her gaze back to Antonio. "Thanks. It's really good. How much do I owe you?"

"This one's on me."

A flush of pink colored her face. Judy must have sensed Marissa's discomfort for she stopped the teasing and changed the subject. "The Easter play was great, Antonio. I never had a chance to tell you. I was talking to Mike recently, and we both agree you should teach drama for a living. Ever thought about it? Mike said he doesn't know how he would've made it through those weeks without you. This is his first year as a children's pastor." She chuckled.

Antonio straightened to a stand. "Yeah, I've thought about it. Mike talked to me, too. And believe me, Judy, if I had the money, I would start my own drama school."

Marissa looked up suddenly. "The dream?"

Antonio gave her a faint smile. "The dream."

Judy looked back and forth between them. Suddenly she snatched her cell phone from her purse and began sliding from the booth. "I just remembered. I was supposed to call my husband. I'll be back soon." With a parting grin she hurried outside, leaving half of her banana split behind to melt.

Antonio quirked his eyebrow in amusement. "Not very subtle, is she?"

"Never," Marissa said with a shy smile. "I've told her that we both agreed we just want to remain friends, but that doesn't stop Judy."

"No, you mean *you* just want to remain friends," he corrected softly. "I'm only going along with the idea for now. But that's not all I want for us."

"It's not?" Her voice came out a shade higher.

"One day I hope to share so much more than friendship with you, Marissa."

A jumble of confused emotions swept through her beautiful eyes—fear, anticipation, and doubt.

"Antonio—"

At the slight warning catch in her voice he lifted his hands. "I'm not talking about today. I'm talking about the future. Tell me truthfully—were you planning to remain single all your life?"

Her eyes widened. "I hadn't given it much thought."

"Hadn't you?" He shook his head and smiled. "You work night and day putting together other people's weddings. You have a natural affinity for children that amazes me. You're generous with your time, giving so much of yourself to others yet expecting so little in return." At this her eyes shifted downward, and he reached over to trace her jaw with his fingertips. Her long lashes flew upward in surprise. "You were designed to be a wife and mother one day, Rissa. It's the natural order of things. You can't tell me you don't think about it sometimes. Not considering the profession you chose."

She swallowed so hard he felt the satiny skin under her jawline pulse with the motion. "Okay, maybe I have thought about it. But what did it get me? An engagement that led to nowhere."

"Not nowhere. Your life isn't over yet. What happened to you during the play was just the beginning, I think. You're like one of those flowers you sell. Partially budded, needing to open its petals to the sun to receive the nurturing light but hesitant to do so." He stroked her cheek in one final, featherlight motion then lowered his hand to his side. "When you do open up, I hope I'm there to witness it. The awakening should be quite something to see."

Sensing, by the stricken look in her eyes, that he'd said too much and she might jump from the booth any moment and race for the door—as quickly as a little gray mouse who'd suddenly found its tail free from the cat's paw—Antonio gave her a half smile, a nod, and headed back to work.

nine

She was wrong. She had to be wrong. Antonio Ramirez couldn't be a thief.

That both he and the cat burglar chose yellow roses was simply some crazy fluke. Maybe Antonio did have a legitimate reason for leaving town on Saturdays and staying gone most of the night. But why had he been so troubled earlier this afternoon when she couldn't give him his requested flower?

With a muffled bang Marissa set the laundry basket of dirty clothes on top of the dryer and opened the washer door. In savage frustration she tossed the items into the hole, one by one.

For the first time since opening the shop, she'd let outside issues interfere with work and had made an embarrassing error. When ordering flowers from her wholesaler in Columbus, something she'd learned to do over the Internet to save time, it slipped her mind that tonight's prom would take more than the usual amount of yellow roses, since gold was a school color. The recent newspaper article about the woman with the black hat from the auction—the winner of Marissa's matching lamp—being the latest victim of the cat burglar had been in the forefront of her thoughts. And Marissa hadn't been able to concentrate on her work. When Linda arrived at the shop to pick up the flowers for the prom, Marissa admitted her error and convinced the girl that sprays of orchid Montecassino—small lilac flowers resembling daisies—would look lovely on some of the tables. She also told her that she would take twenty percent off the total order because of her error, in addition to Linda's employee discount. Linda had eyed Marissa strangely; she had never known her boss to make such a big mistake. But since purple was the school's other color, she went away mollified. Antonio had been another matter altogether.

These past months Marissa had gotten into the habit of putting aside a single rose for him each Saturday. Today, however, in her embarrassed confusion over her careless mistake, she'd given Linda all her yellow roses. Marissa had suggested Antonio purchase a silk one, offering to pull it out of an arrangement, but he declined. Any substitutions offered were equally rejected.

His request that she call another town's florist to see if they had the rose and could deliver it stunned her. All that trouble for one rose? Marissa explained that, even if she did call and ask, and even if they could deliver it, the rose wouldn't get there until Monday, since it was less than an hour away from closing time. And he might not make it to the other shop before five if he chose to drive there either. Antonio had left her store, somber and empty-handed.

"Why can't I stop thinking about him, Sherlock?" she asked the cat, who lay on a braided green rug on the basement floor. "Why do thoughts of him invade night and day?"

Sherlock looked at her with unblinking gold eyes. Marissa sighed and plucked up one of her polyester-silk blouses to put in the protective white net bag she used to wash her delicates. On the rare occasions Antonio didn't show up to buy a flower, there'd been no news of a burglary that night. But Judy was right about one thing. Sometimes, when Antonio bought a rose, no burglary had been reported that night either.

Were his habitual Saturday visits to her shop for the rose coincidental actions that would disprove his guilt, since a theft didn't always follow? Or a cleverly devised scheme to get the law off his trail if they should decide later to investigate his movements these past months? Two things Marissa knew for a fact. At the auction Antonio had met that woman whose jewelry had been burglarized, and he'd seemed very interested in her dazzling necklace. Marissa had caught him eyeing it twice.

With more force than necessary, she grabbed her blue-gray blouse from the basket to put into the net bag. Something flew out of the breast pocket and hit the cement floor with a plastic crackle, startling Sherlock from his doze. He sped to find refuge near the water heater then stared at her from behind the steel contraption, his golden eyes accusing.

"Sorry, old friend." Her gaze went to the blue cylinder wrapped in plastic that lay near the braided rug. Recognizing it as the blue candy cigar a customer gave her months ago, she bent down to pick it up and stared at the white letters on the wrapper, "It's a boy!"

Without warning a need so powerful rose up to overwhelm her, and she thought she might detonate, like a bomb, into millions of unfulfilled pieces. Antonio had been right about one thing when he spoke to her in the ice cream shop last month. She did want a husband, a family.

And she wanted it to be with him.

The cigar snapped in half, the revelation startling. When had she started loving him? And why? He was her suspect; she was his shadow. *But in trailing him,* her mind argued, *you left your self-inflicted solitary existence and stepped out to experience the real world again.*

It was true. If she hadn't followed Antonio, she never would have gone to the woods and discovered the peaceful spot by the stream, which she'd revisited often since that day, marking her path so she wouldn't get lost. If she hadn't wanted to keep tabs on him, she never would have volunteered to help with the Easter play, an act that blessed her in countless areas, the smallest of which—she had stood up in front of a large audience and survived, even with her little misstep at the end. Nor would she have opened up to others, at the same time instigating new friendships with some of the women at church, in her desire to glean what information she could about the mysterious Latin.

In shadowing Antonio, to discover the truth about him, Marissa found a missing part of herself. If nothing of consequence resulted from her sleuthing and no incriminating evidence turned up, at least she would always be thankful to the Father for sending Antonio her way. Her Father did know best. He knew what would prod Marissa out of the protective shell she'd conveniently burrowed under for more than half her life.

"But, Lord, why'd I have to go and fall in love with the guy? I know You often orchestrate things so that many are blessed by one act, and at times we don't understand the why of it all. But surely You knew how I'd come to feel about him. So why send Antonio?"

With Grant, Marissa had liked the idea of being in love and having someone love her. Yet she'd never felt as strongly about him as she did Antonio. When it came to choosing a life mate, her choices were obviously poor ones. First she'd been drawn to a lying womanizer, and now to a probable thief. A charming and considerate and drop-dead gorgeous thief. But still, a man who was, in all likelihood, a thief.

Frowning, she looked down at the broken candy in her tight clutch, wondering. Hoping. Deliberating. Finally, pursing her lips and firming her jaw, she tossed the blue baby cigar in a nearby wastebasket, along with her unattainable desires. She was wrong. She'd told Antonio that everyone could achieve their dreams, if only they pursued them and believed. But some dreams were never meant to be fulfilled. Or they would tear your heart apart, bit by bit.

With jerky movements she dumped a cupful of mild soap into the washer and switched the dials to turn it on. "Be glad you're a cat, Sherlock," she directed to the tiger-striped fur she saw behind a box. "Cats don't have to concern themselves with matters of love."

Walking up the basement stairs, Marissa firmed her resolve. And neither would she.

❧

"You don't know what you're saying," the buzz-headed youth whipped out. The overhead light picked up the blue rose and knife tattoo on his shoulder as he raised a tightly clenched fist. "You think you have all the answers, but you don't. You want a piece of me? Well, here I am."

"Victor!" Antonio raised his hand to stop the sixteen-year-old from spewing his next lines and walked up the stairs at the side of the stage. "I want you to think of me as a member of the opposing gang who's hurt your blood brother. I've just pulled a switchblade on you and am taunting you with what I've done."

Antonio pulled out his pocketknife and bent into an attack crouch, circling Victor slowly, holding out the blunt blade. "You know if you retaliate, you'll hurt the woman you love. The woman you made promises to. My sister. But I just killed your friend. Your best friend. How would you feel? What would you do? Show me." Antonio got into character and began to taunt the youth with words from the script.

Victor narrowed his eyes. This time his lines came out soft and menacing, with the underlying sense of trying to keep his emotions at bay. He opened and clenched his fists, letting them hang by his sides. A nerve in his clean-shaven jaw throbbed.

"Perfect!" Antonio exclaimed. He straightened before Victor forgot himself and tackled him to the floor. "Remember that feeling." He turned to look at the other teenagers. "Keep practicing your lines, all of you—and stand in front of a mirror when you do. That'll help you get the emotion down right. Only four weeks until show time." He glanced at his watch. "That's it for tonight. I'll see you next Saturday."

"Thanks, Mr. R.," Victor said. "We are bad—we are happening!"

Tinman, the nickname of the boy who played one of the gang members in their rendition of *West Side Story*, picked up the chant and high-fived Victor. They both took on what Antonio labeled as their cool, swanky walk out the auditorium doors of the youth center.

"Keep out of trouble," Antonio called, to which Victor raised a hand in acknowledgment without turning around.

The boy was on probation now. Antonio looked after them, wishing he could help every one of these underprivileged kids, though he was doing what he could by keeping them off the streets and involved in drama. *West Side Story*, a modernized Romeo and Juliet tragedy, had been the only play from Antonio's list that appealed to the tough youths, probably because of the presence of gangs in the story. But it did have a message Antonio hoped his group of fourteen would grasp—that fighting wasn't an answer and never solved anything.

"Mr. Ramirez?"

Antonio turned to look at the pretty sixteen year old who played the part of Maria. In the baggy jeans and loose T-shirt, she dressed like one of the guys and hadn't been too thrilled to learn she was to wear a dress for the week-long string of performances they would give. But the girl could act. She was the best performer of the bunch.

"Yes, Leah?"

She twirled her long brown hair and shifted her sneakered feet, her big, dark eyes flirting with him. "My mom can't come to the play. She says that holding down three jobs is enough to ask of anyone, so she can't drive me here early on opening night. Would you come and pick me up?"

By the signals he'd received from the girl this past month, Antonio knew Leah had a crush on him. He didn't want to wound her spirit, but the time had come to let her down gently, without allowing her to realize he knew she liked him. Otherwise he would hurt her pride and probably add another layer of veneer to her hardness. Leah had no father and a mother who showed scant interest. Not wanting the girl to walk to the bus stop after dark, Antonio often gave her a ride home. Leah obviously had read more into his concern than what he offered.

"I'm coming from the other side of town, but I'll find you a ride. You're an important member of this cast, and, speaking as your director only"—he emphasized these last words—"I think you should consider acting school. You have real talent, Leah."

As he spoke, disappointment then hope flickered in her eyes, but almost at once tough regret hardened her features. "Mom would never agree. Things like that cost money."

"I'll talk to her. Maybe we can figure something out." He paused, a thought breezing through his head. "I'll pray about it, too. Maybe the Lord will show us a way." The words slipped out, almost without his realizing it.

She scrunched her brow in curious distaste. "I would've never figured you for one of those Jesus freaks, Mr. Ramirez."

Antonio smiled and headed for the chair holding his things. A few months ago neither would he. Attending church regularly was changing his perspective on a lot of things. He'd witnessed other people's lives being transformed by God, Marissa's included. Maybe it was time to do the same. To surrender. And let God be God in his own life.

Dwelling on the idea, he decided to get together with the

man from Cincinnati soon and talk over the plans. Or maybe he should forget the whole thing and quit while he was ahead.

Antonio shot another glance at his watch, grabbed his things, and walked from the public recreation building to his rental car. Right now he had a rendezvous to keep. And if he didn't move fast, he'd have to put off until next Saturday what he'd planned for tonight.

❧

"Remember what happened to the three blind mice when the farmer's wife got hold of the carving knife?" Marissa hissed the empty threat fueled by weary frustration toward the dark bushes. "Want to be added to that number?"

No meow met her query. No glow of startling night-green, luminescent eyes met the beam of her flashlight.

"Come on, Sherlock. This isn't funny." She felt overtaxed, drained. Her work day had been nonstop, as this whole past month had been. The strain of Easter was always closely followed by the hectic rush of Mother's Day at the florist shop—her two busiest holidays, with Christmas a close third. Add to that the string of brides who chose to get married in May, and she'd barely had time to breathe, even with her employees working as hard as she did. She'd put an old blues record on her ancient phonograph and settled down with a late-night dinner, when she remembered she'd forgotten to get today's mail. She went to retrieve it, and Sherlock had zipped through the open door.

Marissa decided to switch tactics. "If you come out like a good little kitty, I'll give you a pouch of kitty treats. Yummy ones. With liver"—she parted the bushes under Antonio's kitchen window with one hand—"and tuna"—she peeked through the twigs trying to discern if the irregular shape in the dark space by the wall was a cat—"and chicken." She directed her flashlight's beam into the shrubbery.

Twin lights turned into the adjacent drive, spotlighting Marissa in their white beams. Too late, she heard the silent purr of the blue economy car Antonio was now driving and the gravel crunching under his tires. She froze like a deer in the path of an oncoming vehicle and waited for the hunter to pounce.

Antonio stopped his car in the drive and turned off the motor. Marissa had hoped he would have parked in the detached garage. It might have given her the time she needed to make her escape undetected—in case he hadn't seen her.

"Marissa?"

Another hope shot to the dust.

"What are you doing over there? It's"—he glanced at his watch—"after two in the morning."

Marissa switched off the flashlight since he'd kept the headlights on, though thankfully they were pointed at the garage and no longer blinding her. "Sherlock's loose again."

"Really."

"Yes, really," she shot back irritably. "Why else would I be out here in the middle of the night, searching through your bushes, with only my house shoes on?" Too late. She wished she hadn't drawn attention to her footwear—the gag gift of pink, fuzzy bunny slippers Judy had given her last Christmas.

His gaze lowered, and his brow lifted in casual amusement. "You couldn't find your shoes?"

Oh, what was the use of explaining the heels she'd worn today were too high and thin to keep from sinking into the soft ground? She often put on her comfortable slippers after work. But let him think she was a nut case. He probably did anyway.

"Just forget it," she groused, turning back to the bushes and clicking on her flashlight.

The car's twin beams disappeared, the blackness again swallowing up the area, and she heard the rustle of his footsteps in the grass as he came up behind her. "I'm sorry. I'll help."

Marissa didn't argue. The sooner the dumb animal was found, the sooner she could go home, lock her door, and pretend this latest humiliation never happened.

"I think I might know where he could be. May I?" Antonio held out his hand for the flashlight. Marissa grudgingly gave it to him and followed him to the other side of the house.

A honeydew slice of a waning moon on a tablecloth of blue-black sky was all that guided them, besides the flashlight beam that Antonio swung erratically from side to side. Not one, but two sets of glowing green eyes shaped like lemon drops suddenly caught the light, appearing to hover a few inches above the grass, licorice-colored because of the night.

Marissa really did need to eat.

Spotting a patch of white fur, she paused in startled disbelief. "Snowflake?"

Hearing its name, the all-white cat let out a mournful *meowww* then slowly moved from the haven of bushes toward Marissa and Antonio. Antonio crouched and held out his hand, letting Snowflake tentatively sniff it. The cat began furiously licking his fingers.

"Tuna sandwich," Antonio explained over his shoulder to Marissa. With his other hand he set down the flashlight and picked up the cat that never ceased from giving Antonio's hand a bath. Marissa reclaimed her flashlight and trained it on the cat. The once sleek fur was matted, and what looked like cockleburs stuck in her coat.

"The poor thing is probably half-starved," Marissa said. "Snowflake belongs to the previous owners of your house, the Kincaids, but she disappeared the day before they moved. The whole family searched, but no one could find her. The kids were devastated." Marissa reached out to pet the cat, which lay like a rescued survivor in Antonio's arms. "I have no idea how she made it through this past winter. It was mild, but we still had snow. You've been through a hard time of it, haven't you, Girl?"

Snowflake burrowed her ears and face into Marissa's palm, obviously starved for affection, as well as food.

"She probably somehow found a way into my basement from outside," Antonio said. "I heard the usual nighttime sounds of thumps and creaks down there once in awhile but didn't give it much thought."

"I'll take her home with me and Sherlock. If you'll give me the number of your real estate agent, I'll phone and see if they can get a message to the Kincaids. They didn't move too far from here if I remember right."

Marissa focused her attention and flashlight on the other pair of glowing emerald eyes staring at her from the bushes and moved that way. "Sherlock, you're a good kitty, and I take back every mean thing I said. All this time you were trying to tell me you'd found Snowflake, weren't you?"

Sherlock didn't blink, but Marissa thought she saw his mouth turn up. Did cats smile?

She reached out and pulled him from the bushes. He resisted, digging his back claws into the earth. "It's okay, Boy," she grunted. "We're taking your girlfriend home with us."

Suddenly he broke free and raced toward the woods. Marissa shot up and started after him—stepping on one of the long, floppy ears of her clunky bunny slippers. Her palms flew out to save her face from smashing into the grass.

Antonio was instantly by her side. "You okay?" She nodded, and he thrust Snowflake at her. "You hold this one. I'll get yours."

Snowflake, however, lost all her docility and now seemed edgy, nervous about these nutty people, Marissa was sure, or maybe scared of the huge pink rabbit feet. A bolt of energy seemed to zap the feline, and she struggled to get loose.

Marissa soon discovered this cat had all her claws. "Youch!"

Snowflake jumped gracefully to the ground and dashed in the direction Sherlock had taken. Antonio soon came back, catless.

"I have an idea," he said. "Come with me."

Marissa followed him into his kitchen. He opened the window wide then brought the can opener from the other side of the room and plugged it into a socket nearby, setting the opener on the window ledge. Grabbing two cans of tuna, he put each underneath the magnet one at a time and pushed down the lever. A loud mechanic whir filled the kitchen.

He gave the smelly cans to Marissa. "Dump these into two bowls and set them on the back porch. You'll find the bowls in that cabinet by the fridge and the silverware in the drawer underneath."

While Marissa scooped the flaked fish out into plastic containers, Antonio continued to work the lever at intervals. Marissa hoped the sound would carry to the woods, heralding the cats. She turned on the back porch light and opened the screen door to set the bowls outside then rejoined Antonio who was still making noise with the opener.

"Ah, Houston—we have success," he said at last.

Marissa looked over his shoulder and out the window, searching the lighted porch area. Amid the cheery black-eyed Susans and relaxed purple coneflowers, whose shape resembled upside-down badminton birdies, a patch of white and one of tabby raced toward Antonio's house. He beckoned with his finger, and Marissa followed him to the back door. Through the screen they saw both cats devouring the food from the two bowls.

"One more thing." Antonio silently opened the door and grabbed the first cat and bowl, setting them inside, then did the same with the other. Sherlock didn't even ruffle a hair in protest. He seemed quite content to let Antonio handle him.

"Really I should just go on and take them home," Marissa argued. "As you pointed out earlier, it's late."

"Let the white one finish her meal," Antonio suggested. "She looks hungry."

Marissa glanced at Snowflake. As she sat, hunched over, Marissa could see the cat's scapula bones were more obvious through the fur than Sherlock's. "Okay. Just until Snowflake finishes eating."

"If you want to wash up, the bathroom is down the hall to the right," Antonio offered, and Marissa looked at herself for the first time.

Her skirt was peppered with grass and dirt from her fall, and her palms stung. Looking at them, she saw they were red.

"Are you all right?" Antonio gently grasped her wrists and surveyed the inside of her hands.

"Of course." She jerked both hands away. "I'll just go wash up," she said as an excuse.

When she returned, Snowflake was still eating. For a half-starved cat, she was sure going about her meal in a dainty fashion. Sherlock had finished and now lay stretched out a few feet from the bowl on the cool floor.

"Can I ask a favor, Rissa?"

Antonio's soft voice stirred the jarring silence that had put her nerves on edge. Marissa turned warily to find him standing close. Too close for her peace of mind.

"You can ask, but I'm not sure I'll grant it." She couldn't back up because the wall stood in the way.

He grinned. "Fair enough. My rental's been acting up—crazy, huh? I'm having trouble starting it, but until I can trade it in for another, I don't have dependable wheels. Can I ride with you to church tomorrow?"

She blinked in surprise. "Sure."

At her reaction his grin grew lopsided, but his eyes were sober. "Did you think my requested favor was going to involve something immoral?"

"No, of course not." Heat bathed her cheeks and forehead.

"Yes, you did." He sobered. "I'll admit I haven't always led a pure life, Marissa, and I'm not proud of it. But I've changed."

"That's nice. But you don't have to tell me all this," she whispered.

"I want to."

Marissa felt herself grow wondrously lost in the liquid-brown eyes that now shimmered like dark, exotic pools of moonlit-laced water. She moved her head back the scant distance it took for it to touch the wall.

"Why?" Her word was a mere puff of air.

"Because I don't want the past to stand between us." He lowered his head and kissed her tenderly, taking her breath away. "Because I want you to know what you're getting into," he murmured when he raised his head. "But most of all because I think I'm falling in love with you."

She gasped and jerked backward, her shoulders hitting the wall.

"Marissa?" His voice came out hoarse.

"I don't know what to say," she whispered.

"Then don't say anything. Just please, whatever you do, don't tell me there's no hope for us either."

This time when he kissed her, Marissa kissed him back. For mindless seconds she enjoyed nothing but Antonio's lips on hers, the security of his strong arms around her. She broke away and stared, shocked by her lack of sound judgment. What was she doing?

"I have to go," she blurted.

He nodded solemnly. "I know. I'll carry one of the cats."

He released her and scooped up Sherlock. Marissa stood

still a moment, to gather her bearings, then picked up Snowflake, who'd finally finished her meal. Antonio didn't seem the least bit affected by their kiss, while Marissa's heart still pounded and her skin tingled. But then—of course. He already had a girlfriend, didn't he?

How could he tell her he loved her when he apparently was showing his affection toward someone else? Or, if the curio cabinet wasn't for his girl, then for whom had he bought it?

Cradling Snowflake to her chest, Marissa followed Antonio across the street. She lightly pressed her lips against the cat's soft white head, murmuring comforting words into its ear, though she wasn't sure if it was for Snowflake's benefit or if she was the one who needed the reassurance. Antonio had lied to her before. Well, not really lied, but he'd withheld the truth about being an actor and hadn't given an explanation of why he'd done it. Was he withholding the truth about other things, too?

Daily Marissa rode a mental seesaw of believing Antonio was a decent guy to thinking he must be a thief. Once again the board tipped on the negative side, out of his favor, leaving Marissa determined to clear up something tonight. Of course, she couldn't come straight out and ask, "Are you a cat burglar?" Any self-respecting thief would deny it, and she might even scare him away. Whether he was guilty of the crime or not, his answer to such a question would undoubtedly be a no. But she could ask him about the other matter troubling her.

At her porch she opened the door and set Snowflake down on the polished wooden planks. The cat hesitated then moved further inside the front room. The phonograph was making a constant, irritating, nails-down-the-chalkboard *skritching* noise, minus the squeak, the needle having reached the end of the record. At least the static sound didn't scare the cat back outside.

"Maybe you should invest in a leash," Antonio joked as he handed her Sherlock, and she set him inside also.

She closed the door, her hand still on the latch, and gave Antonio a level stare. "Before you go, I want you to answer a question for me, and I want the truth."

A puzzled frown crossed his brow. "Okay."

"Do you or do you not have a girlfriend?"

He stared at her awhile, his eyes solemn. "I do not."

It was on the tip of her tongue to blurt out, "Then who are all those yellow roses for?" But of course she didn't.

He hesitated a few seconds before he continued. "I understand how your ex-fiancé hurt you, Marissa, and that trust is a hard issue for you right now. But, let me assure you, I'm a one-woman man. I saw my mother's pain and what she went through, and I could never hurt a woman as my father hurt her. If there were someone else, I wouldn't have kissed you as I did. I'm not as bad as all that."

"Thank you for telling me," Marissa said hollowly. "I should go in now. Morning will be here before you know it."

Again he looked confused. "I'll be ready to go at 9:45. Okay?"

"Fine." She gave him a faint smile before heading into the house and closing the door. Inside she inhaled a deep breath to pull herself together, though she felt like falling apart. No matter what his answer, Antonio was still her suspect—now more so than ever, since he denied having a girl to give the flowers to. His mother was dead, his aunt and other relatives in Spain. Since he never mentioned any other family, Marissa assumed there was none.

The mental seesaw slammed down on the side pointing to his guilt, tossing Marissa off into a sandy sea of regret. To protect herself and her town, to do what was right, she had no choice but to proceed with her amateur investigation. Even if it felt as if her heart were breaking in two.

ten

Late Friday evening a week later, Marissa filled out her order for flowers, sending it via the Internet. Then she prepared the correspondence that needed to be mailed out the next day, including new orders for the seamstress concerning next year's wedding gowns. One was for an Edwardian-style wedding, the other a picture of a medieval gown. She'd never coordinated a medieval wedding and looked forward to the challenge.

Picking up the Griswald folder, she opened it and carefully skimmed the detailed checklist of all the things needing to be done before the ceremony on Sunday evening. She was just fitting a numbered cassette into her tape player, to double-check the classical piped-in reception music the girl had requested, when she heard someone pounding loudly on one of the outside doors to the shops.

Marissa froze for a heartbeat then looked over her shoulder to her office entrance. She couldn't see anything beyond the barrier that divided the bridal area and florist. Who could be demanding to be let in so long after closing time? Except for the fluorescent lamp in her office and the one inside the refrigerated doors with the flowers, the place was dark, the overhead lights having been turned off in both shops. Marissa couldn't think of any floral emergency that would constitute such behavior, unless it was one of her clients, an emotional girl named Misty who bordered on near hysteria most of the time and whose wedding was next weekend. Yet seeing the place was dark, wouldn't she come by in the morning, which wasn't all that far away? Or was

Marissa's office light apparent to someone standing outside looking in?

The knock came again, this time quicker and at the other door, as though the person issuing it had grown impatient or frantic. Marissa inhaled a deep, steadying breath and made her way slowly to the front. Suddenly she felt vulnerable, though working late at the shop never had bothered her before. Wadleyville boasted of being a quiet town with a low crime rate. Yet lately she felt about as safe as a wary rabbit trapped in a thicket maze with an unpredictable hunter. For weeks she'd waited for Antonio to make his move. The burglaries only occurred when the victims were absent from their homes so she'd left her car behind the closed garage door and kept any lights off that could be seen from the street, giving the appearance of not being home. Her little town wasn't wallowing in wealth as other neighborhoods the cat burglar had struck, but she'd tempted him with her costly jewelry, and he'd seemed interested enough.

A man's figure stood outside the plate-glass window of the florist shop. In the light from the street lamp behind him, Marissa could see it was drizzling outside. The lamp's glow outlined his form, and a few cautious steps later she could tell it was Antonio. Glad to see it wasn't a stranger, she turned on a small, decorative lamp on the counter. She hesitated only a moment before she undid the bolt and opened the door.

"Marissa!" he exclaimed. "Are you all right?"

She furrowed her brow. "Why shouldn't I be?"

"Judy's been trying to call you for hours—both at your home and here at your shop—and when she couldn't get through, she was worried and called me." He looked over his shoulder and waved at a brown car sitting nearby whose headlights beamed onto the wet street. Slowly the car pulled out from the curb and drove away.

"Who was that?" Marissa asked, vaguely wondering how Judy had Antonio's number when Marissa herself didn't.

"One of our neighbors. He dropped me off. I couldn't find my keys, and he was heading to town." Without another word Antonio took hold of Marissa's elbow, steering her back into the store. He went directly to the phone sitting on the counter. Even before he adjusted it, Marissa saw that the receiver was slightly off the hook. A mistake anyone could have made as busy as it became just before closing time. He waited several seconds then picked up the receiver and put the phone to his ear. She watched as he pulled a scrap of paper from his pocket and punched in a string of numbers.

"Judy? She's here, safe and sound. I'll let you talk to her." He handed the phone to Marissa, who was beginning to feel like a chastened child who'd stayed out after dark.

"Hi, Judy!" she brightly said into the mouthpiece.

"What are you doing, going and scaring everyone half to death?" her friend shot back. "This *would* be the one night Glen took the car. But let me tell you I was about ready to walk down there in the rain. I was picturing all sorts of awful things that could've happened to you. Your silly murder mysteries have finally gotten to me! But, thank God, I got Antonio's number from Mike. Anyway, what I wanted to tell you, is that the Kincaids told my friend Beth, Antonio's realtor, that they'd like to drive up to Wadleyville Monday to pick up their cat. They were excited to hear Snowflake had been found and tried to call you at your house—Beth did, too—but of course you're never home lately."

Marissa waited for Judy to wind down. When her friend was excited, she almost always rambled. "Relax, Judy. I'm fine. Tell Beth that Monday is fine, too. The Kincaids can drop by the shop when they get here, and I'll take time off to run with them to my house so they can get Snowflake."

"Will do." Judy paused, probably collecting breath for another round. "You know, Marissa, you sure have a jewel in that man. Whatever you do, don't let him go."

Surprised at the soft, short words when she was expecting another spiel of them, Marissa didn't have to ask whom Judy was talking about. She knew. "Thanks, Judy."

As Marissa hung up the receiver, making sure it was solidly on the hook this time, her gaze went to Antonio, who stared at a nearby flower arrangement. His hair glistened with droplets, his clothes looked thrown on, as if he'd grabbed them in the dark—a gray sweatshirt and dark brown dress trousers—and his features were drawn and tight. His forefinger touched the petal of a flower.

"What does this one mean?" he asked, though it didn't sound as if he really cared.

Marissa looked at the oleander, a vague sense of unease prickling her.

When she didn't respond, Antonio looked up.

"It means 'beware,'" she said after a moment, shaking off the eerie, omen like feeling. "Listen—I'm sorry about your having to come out like this and on such a miserable night, too."

"I don't mind, but where's your car?"

"My car?" Remembrance dawned. "Oh, I had to run an errand earlier this afternoon, and when I got back someone had taken my spot. I parked around the side of the building.

"I got worried when I didn't see it. I wasn't sure what had happened to you."

"You were worried about me?" Marissa asked wonderingly.

"Of course." He took the few steps toward her. "I care about you, Rissa."

How could chill bumps dance across her arms when she felt so fuzzy-warm inside? She didn't know how to respond.

"Do you have a lot of work to do yet?" he asked.

"I think I've pretty well covered what needs to be done tonight."

"In that case, would you mind dropping me off when you go home? Also, if it wouldn't be too much trouble"—he grinned boyishly—"could we stop on the way and pick up some hamburgers? Experiencing panic always makes me hungry afterward, and I'm behind on grocery shopping."

"Sure." Why did his smile always produce the effect of making her feel topsy-turvy inside, like a shaken snow globe? "I'll finish closing up and grab my things. It shouldn't take more than five minutes."

As she shut down her computer, Marissa thought of what a caring and thoughtful man Antonio was. He hadn't needed to come to her shop, in the rain and late at night, but he'd done it. Judy was right. Marissa was letting her imagination get the best of her. No man so considerate could be a thief.

She turned off her office light and walked to the front, her rainy-day loafers she'd worn with her pantsuit making no noise on the tiles. She stopped short at hearing Antonio talking on the phone with someone.

"I've been trying to reach you for hours," he ground out, his voice low. "I left a message for you to call this afternoon. So what's the plan?" A pause. "Are you sure? There's no other way?" A beseeching thread was sewn into the angry dismay of his voice. "Surely there's something else that can be done. Do we really have to resort to *that*?"

Marissa jumped when he slammed the counter with his fist in a gavel-like motion. The fierce action seemed to drain him, and she heard him exhale a long, weary sigh as he lowered his head and swiped his hand down the back of it, gripping his neck.

"Fine. Right," he muttered. "Then I guess there's no option

left but to do her in. You do what you have to do. I'll do the rest. I'll take care of it tomorrow."

Shock froze Marissa to the spot. Horror and disbelief clutched her stomach with sharp talons, making her dizzy and sick. When he moved to hang up the receiver, she turned and hurriedly retraced her steps. Her mind hummed, and her body trembled. She had to think. What should she do? Had she heard right?

Not only was Antonio a thief, as she had feared, but he had a partner—and they were about to commit *murder?* Marissa had watched enough detective flicks to know that to do someone in was to kill a person. Who? What unsuspecting, poor soul had Antonio and his accomplice targeted? A wash of cold terror swept through her, chilling her to her very marrow. *Dear God, please no. . .*was it her? But why? *Beware. . .*the silent message of the oleander echoed in her brain.

"Are you ready to go?"

Antonio's voice coming from directly behind Marissa made her jump, and she swung around to face him. "What?" Her purse bumped a silk flower basket, knocking it off the shelf. Decorative pebbles rained onto the floor. She knelt down to clean the mess, though her hands were shaking. "Oh, sure. I'm ready when you are. Just let me get this first."

He knelt to help her scrape the loose pebbles together and drop them back into the basket. In his hands the crimson pebbles shimmered like drops of blood. She hastily looked away and stood, watching as he replaced the flower arrangement on the shelf.

"Are you okay? You seem upset." His abrupt Jekyll-and-Hyde switch, from quietly furious to sweetly concerned, was unsettling. But then he was an actor. He knew how to play a part well.

"I'm fine," Marissa muttered. "I just got a case of the

willies—that's all." *How can I be anything but upset after what I just learned about you?* She felt like screaming out the words, but fear of what else she might blurt kept her bucking emotions on a tight rein.

He looked at her strangely, as if she were the one acting out of the ordinary. "Okay, then. Let's get out of here. I'm not sure how late the fast food restaurant is open, but I know the drive-thru stays open 'til eleven."

Marissa led the way to the door, locking it once they were outside. A glimmer of reality shone behind the dark shade of mistrust that had slammed down over her thoughts. If she was the intended victim, why had Antonio told his partner that he would "take care of it tomorrow" when he had the opportunity to "do her in" tonight?

Of course, she answered her own mental question. The neighbor. And Judy. Both knew that Antonio was with her. Which meant that for the time being Marissa was safe.

She wished that thought did more to comfort her. She could scarcely feel anything beyond stunned disbelief that the man she'd unwisely grown to love was worse than a cat burglar. He was a cold-blooded killer. Her heart argued the point, but she could see no other explanation for his terse words on the phone.

He had fooled them all.

❧

If he didn't know better, Antonio would say he was in the car alone. Marissa was unusually quiet. He looked over at her in a reflex action, to assure himself that she was behind the wheel even though logically he knew she was. In the blue-white lights of the fast-food parking lot, he couldn't see much, but he could tell she was frowning.

"Don't you like your chicken sandwich?" he asked. He had insisted on buying her something, against the idea of eating his two double-patty cheeseburgers, large fries, and a big soda in front of someone who had nothing.

"Sure. It's great." She took a bite and chewed, adding to the one small nibble she'd taken from the bun minutes ago.

"What's wrong, Marissa?"

"Nothing's wrong. It's just been a long day, and I need to get home." She set her sandwich down in the crackly yellow paper and wrapped it back up. With a twist of the keys that dangled from the ignition, the car roared to life, and she quickly backed out of the lot.

Antonio wrapped up the rest of his second sandwich and stuck it in the white paper sack. He didn't want to risk eating while she was driving. Some of the fixings might fall out of his burger, and in the dark he wouldn't see where they landed. Or, worse case scenario, he might choke on his food with the crazy turns she made on the rain-slick roads.

"Marissa! Watch out!" Antonio yelled, clutching the dashboard as they careened around a corner too fast.

They went into a quarter spin and landed on the other side of the median. She gasped and righted the car. He was thankful there was no traffic this late at night, no car in sight at all. He pictured the car hydroplaning at any moment and tensed for the event, certain they would end up going over the hillside yet. Was she experiencing a flashback of some deep-seated desire to be a race-car driver?

"Would you like me to drive?" Antonio asked, bottling up what he really wanted to say.

"No. Sorry. I had my mind on something else and wasn't thinking. I'm really not a bad driver. I've had only two tickets in my entire life, but that was back in high school."

And that was supposed to reassure him? He muttered something noncommittal, keeping on the lookout, intently scouting the road for any possible hazards so as to warn her far in advance. To his relief the car slowed down significantly, and he relaxed. She came to a stoplight but sat there several seconds after the red orb disappeared.

"Light's green," Antonio prodded, thankful no one was behind them.

"What? Oh." She stepped on the accelerator a little too hard, and the tires spun.

Antonio stared at her. He knew she was a good driver. She'd taken him to church last Sunday. But tonight she was acting like a nervous driver's ed. student behind the wheel for the first time. What was wrong with her? Ever since she'd come out of her office, she'd been acting strangely, as though something was bothering her. She hadn't been that happy to see him tonight; he could sense that by her behavior.

Earlier suspicions teased his mind, bringing to the forefront other unexplained occurrences and curious facts regarding the mystery of Marissa, but he forced all doubts away.

He was glad when they made it to her gravel drive in one piece.

Marissa jumped out of the car with a quick "G'night" and headed for her porch. Antonio raised his brows at her hurried departure then noticed she had left her briefcase on the back seat. He grabbed it.

"Marissa—wait!" he called as he exited her car. He lowered his voice, realizing most of their neighbors were probably asleep. "You forgot this."

She halted at the top of the porch and turned. He hurried her way but noticed the quick, little backward step she took when he reached the steps and took the first stair.

"Is something bothering you?" he asked.

"I'm just tired. I haven't been getting a lot of sleep."

"I know." The porch light wasn't on, but he could tell her eyes had widened, and he hastened to add, "I noticed your lights have been going out later than usual."

"You've been watching me?" she whispered.

"No. That came out wrong." He gave up trying to get what he meant across to her and closed the distance between them, handing her the brown leather case. "Here. I should go."

He hesitated after she'd taken it. "I worry about you, Marissa. You haven't been yourself lately. If you ever need to talk, as we did on Easter, I'm just down the street, remember? Your cat can show you the way if you forget." She didn't crack a smile at his little joke, and Antonio decided it was past time to leave.

Knowing he shouldn't, but feeling the need to offer some kind of reassurance and wanting to touch her, he bent down to kiss her troubled forehead. He heard her indrawn gasp. When he straightened, he saw a shimmer of wetness in her eyes.

"Marissa?"

She only shook her head and turned to slip the key into the lock. After struggling with it for some time without success, Antonio reached for the key ring. "Let me try."

She hesitated then drew her hand away. The lock was rusty, and it took a few swift, hard jiggles; but finally Antonio got it to turn. As he handed the key ring back to her, he said, "I have some WD-40 I'll bring over after church on Sunday, and we'll see if that doesn't take care of the problem. I'm not great on fixing cars, but I'm not bad for a handyman. And I'm good at catching cats, too," he added with a grin.

She looked at him for a few unsmiling seconds then reclaimed her keys. "Why'd you have to be so nice?" she asked sadly before stepping into her house and closing the door.

Meaning he was supposed to be cruel? Perplexed, Antonio stared at the spot where he'd last seen her then shook his head and walked home. Women. They were hard enough to understand sometimes, but with Marissa a man needed a woman's behavioral-dictionary-encyclopedia. If there was such a thing, Antonio would be the first to invest in one. He wanted to know Marissa, to know what made her happy or sad. To know what pushed the wrong buttons and what pushed the right ones. And especially to know what it would take to put that glow on her face, like the one he'd seen when she discovered the stream in the woods that day.

For a girl who appeared to be doing all right financially, she didn't seem all that happy. But then, after what she'd been through, that was no surprise. He thought about the jerk she'd been engaged to and what a loser he must be. Her words came back to Antonio, a whisper in the night.

Why'd you have to be so nice?

Like a spotlight suddenly illuminating a dark stage, it hit him. She must be starting to care for him and was fighting it because of what loser-boy had done to her! The thought pleased Antonio but was worrisome, too. Before they could take their relationship to another level, he needed more funds. He didn't want her ever to think she had to take care of him. Like a wealthy ex-girlfriend in L.A. had wanted to do. Treating Antonio as she did her award-winning pedigree, a show-and-tell item to be exhibited to her snobby friends at parties. That relationship, if it could be called that, lasted two weeks before Antonio had had enough.

But Marissa. . .Marissa was a prize to be treasured and adored. She deserved nothing less. Antonio just wished he could figure out what was troubling her. He didn't think the revelation of any feelings she might have toward him would drive her behavior to such theatrical lengths—to the point of paranoia. What then?

Letting himself inside the house, he made a decision. He would call the man from Cincinnati tomorrow and accept his offer. Once he had enough money, Antonio could consider approaching Marissa as more than just a neighbor or a friend. The question was whether he could convince her that the time had come in their relationship to take that chance. If he was right about her parting words and what they meant, he could. But if he was wrong, he risked scaring her away and losing her for good.

eleven

Saturday dawned hot and humid but overcast, with rain more than likely to hit. Marissa donned a black linen pantsuit to match the dreary weather and her mood. After Easter she had decided to implement her wardrobe with cheery colors, to celebrate her reemergence into life. But today she felt no joy, no victory. Today she picked a shade that matched the hollow emptiness inside her soul.

Antonio was a killer. Yet, even knowing that, her foolish heart continued to love him. She'd almost broken down last night after that sweet kiss to her brow, after hearing his caring words, and bawled like a baby, wanting to strike his chest with her fists and repeatedly cry out, "Why?" Wanting to shake some sense back into him. Wanting to pull him inside with her and lock him into a room so he couldn't go through with the premeditated murder.

Playing detective was a job only for the thick-skinned, which she wasn't. Once again life dealt her a cruel hand. The question was, should she withdraw and fold? Or see this deadly game through to the end? Of course she had no choice. Some poor soul was the targeted victim, and she alone knew it. Late into the night she'd sat huddled on her couch and battled the issue, finally coming to the conclusion that she couldn't be the one they were after. It just didn't make sense for Antonio to seek her out and be so kind to her, show such genuine concern, then bump her off the next day. Then, too, he could have stolen her inherited jewels on any evening she wasn't home, since he was her neighbor. Not just on a Saturday night when the cat burglar struck. There was no reason to kill her to get to them.

At the shop Marissa pulled Linda aside when she arrived for work and took her to the office. "Let me know when Antonio gets here. I want you to wait on him. I'll be back here, working in my office all day and will be leaving later to run an errand."

Linda looked at her strangely. "Okay. You're the boss, but I sure hope it won't be like last Saturday. Maybe you should hire my cousin, too. She loves flowers—she's the one who taught me how to do arrangements—and we could sure use the help."

"I'll think about it."

Linda looked at the overhead clock then pulled a piece of well-chewed blue gum from her mouth and tossed it into the trash. "Time to open up shop." Marissa watched the teenager move to the door to unlock it for the start of the business day. A glance into the bridal area assured her that Gladys was doing the same. Marissa closed her office door and waited.

Hours ticked slowly by. Antonio was late.

Marissa was in the middle of scanning a client's file, experiencing the horrible feeling that she'd forgotten to do something important, when the summons came.

"He's here," Linda whispered through the door she'd partially opened.

"For a yellow rose?" Marissa asked.

"Yeah. Did you want to talk to him?"

"No! Not now. You go ahead and take care of him. I put his rose in the workroom cooler. It's already wrapped."

"O–kaay." Linda sounded puzzled, but Marissa didn't enlighten her. Once the teenager left, Marissa grabbed her purse and headed for the delivery door. She slipped out the back, into the narrow alley, and hurried to her car.

An eternity seemed to elapse before she saw Antonio's new

rental pull away from the curb. She ducked out of sight as he drove past, waited a few moments, then straightened and turned the wheel to follow. She hoped he didn't look into his rearview mirror and spot her, but to be on the safe side she stayed as far behind as she could without losing him completely. When he left the Wadleyville city limits, she thanked the Lord that she remembered to put gas in the tank yesterday, just in case this turned out to be a long drive.

Twenty minutes out of town, he pulled onto a little-used rural road, well shaded by red maples. Marissa hesitated. No traffic appeared to be on the road, which strengthened the chances of his seeing her, but what choice did she have? Someone's life was in danger.

They traveled a few miles, into Bolton; then he turned off onto another road, which seemed to go on forever. Finally he turned right onto another shaded lane. This one appeared to be someone's ranch; Marissa could see horses and sheep grazing. A mammoth one-story white and blue building, with wings going off in three directions, sat at the end of a curved drive. Hardwood trees and pines provided an abundance of shade, and Marissa could see a group of elderly people sitting in lawn chairs near a stone fountain close to the nucleus of the building. A sign nearby read, "Shady Hills Retirement Center."

Marissa blinked. Surely he wouldn't target one of the elderly! Just from the grounds she could see that the place was posh, and she imagined that only the very wealthy could afford to live in such a location. He parked his car, and Marissa slid into a space on the opposite side of the lot, set the brake, turned off her motor, and scrunched down, hoping he hadn't seen her.

A minute later a knuckle tapped on her driver's side window.

She groaned and straightened, looking toward him. So much for her amateur sleuthing.

The look on his face was priceless—a mixture of disbelief, confusion, and despair. She opened the door, and he stepped aside so she could get out.

"Marissa, what're you doing here?" His words were tense, abrupt.

"How'd you know it was me?"

"The 'With God All Things Are Possible' bumper sticker on the rear end of your car was a dead giveaway."

Well, maybe she'd flunked Detective 101, but she could still try to talk sense into him. As a Christian, as a good citizen, she had to do what she could to stop him.

"Don't go through with this, Antonio. Please." At the blankness covering his face, she explained, "I know all about the plan. I overheard you talking last night. Nothing is worth the loss of a life. And you'll get prison if you go through with this. Is that what you want? To throw away your dream and rot in some cramped cell—all for a stupid jewel?"

He stared at her as if she'd crawled off the back of a UFO. "I have no idea what you're talking about, but I have to go now. We'll talk later." He stepped away, but she grabbed his muscled arm, and for the first time she noticed he was holding the yellow rose.

"You do so know what I'm talking about!" she raised her voice to a higher pitch. A few of the elderly loungers turned to look their way. "And I'm not going to let you do it. I'll call security if I have to, if you won't listen to reason. I care about you, too, Antonio, and I'm not going to just stand here and do nothing while you throw your life away!"

Her declaration was made so loudly, so vehemently that two women strolling past the entrance with walkers stopped to stare.

Antonio cast a nervous glance at the gawking residents and grabbed Marissa's upper arm. "Come on then," he said quietly. "But I really wish you hadn't followed me here."

Marissa just bet he did! The thought that he might use her as his hostage, to get out of town if he should get caught, branded itself across her mind, and she reconsidered the intelligence of spouting such hasty words.

They walked together through an automatic door, which an elderly man moved toward. He gave them an open-eyed owl look as he shuffled past them.

"Antonio, you're hurting my arm!"

Instantly the pressure slackened though he didn't release her as she'd hoped.

"Please, if you let me go, I won't tell anyone about how you were involved, when I call the police. But I implore you, I beg you—please don't go through with this!"

Antonio nodded to an African-American woman wearing a crisp pink linen pantsuit and talking on the phone, obviously one of the workers, but never relaxed his hurried pace down the plush-carpeted hallway. The woman stared at them, one dark brow raised.

"Marissa, believe me—we'll talk more about this later. Right now I'm late. And trying to make sense out of whatever it is you're saying is putting me on edge."

"Then you're meeting him here?"

He looked at her sharply. "Who?"

"The man on the phone, of course." Or was it a woman? She had never thought of his accomplice as other than a man, but some women engaged in murder, too. And that would explain the rose. "Or is it a she you're meeting up with? Is it one of the workers here?"

Marissa almost felt sorry for Antonio. Her bramble-tangled, panic-laced phrases were even getting hard for her to understand.

Antonio gave a terse shake of his head, about at the end of

his rope from the way his jaw jerked and his lips thinned. They stopped at the entrance to a sunroom. He released her arm and took a deep breath. "After you." His words were short. The glint in his eye didn't tolerate refusal.

Huge gleaming windows looked out onto rolling lawns and filled almost every available space on the pastel yellow walls. Lush greenery exploded in sweeps of ferns, twining ivies, and pink-tinged elephant ears from planters all around the sunny room. In a white bamboo chair, an elderly Spanish woman sat, wearing a scarlet-red and ivory flowered top and charcoal-gray slacks. Her dark eyes sparkled upon catching sight of Antonio. Thick black hair was looped around the back of her head and was lightly streaked with silver.

"Antonio, *mi querido*," she exclaimed softly, holding her veined hands out to him. Jeweled rings flashed on almost every finger. She stood with ease, as graceful as a gazelle, though she was as tiny as a bird. Marissa was surprised to note that the woman was even shorter than her own diminutive height.

The Spanish lady took one of Antonio's hands in a loving grip, and he moved the hand to slip it around her frail waist, bending to kiss her dusky cheek. When he straightened, he handed her the rose. "I'm sorry I'm so late, Grandmother."

"Grandmother?" Marissa gasped.

Both of them looked at her, and she now saw the resemblance.

"She's your grandmother," Marissa said a little more loudly as the light of understanding dawned.

"Yes. Marissa Hughes, I'd like you to meet Maria Carlotta Rodriguez de Milano Porter. Grandmother—"

"Not *the* Carlotta Milano?" Marissa felt her cheeks grow warm at the monumental error she'd made, but her brain still seemed to work and clicked the familiar names together. The face matched, too, still beautiful, almost ageless, after what must be more than sixty years off screen. "The actress?"

Antonio looked surprised and gave his grandmother an apologetic look. "I'm sorry. I didn't think she'd know you."

"It's all right, Antonio," the woman said with a recognizable but faded Spanish accent, her curious eyes on Marissa. "Yes, I was an actress. I played on stage and in several motion pictures before I met my Frederick. We had a farm not far from here." The liquid-black eyes grew a little sad. "My Frederick, he died three years ago. I came to this place to be near him, when I could no longer run the farm."

"I'm sorry." Marissa hesitated only a second, unable to contain her excitement. "I remember seeing you in *A Rose in the Night*. You played the part of Catherine's sister—Alana— and I thought you were the killer for half the movie. You were wonderful!" Marissa realized she sounded like a sappy, tongue-tied fan, but she couldn't seem to help herself. Carlotta Milano had been one of her favorite secondary actresses, and she always wondered why she'd never been cast as the main star.

Carlotta's eyes brightened. "You watched that—and remember me?" She turned her gaze to Antonio. "You should have brought her here before this, especially since she will be my new granddaughter. She's even sweeter than you said. And she has good taste. Both in movies and in men." Carlotta chuckled.

"Grandmother, I never said that Marissa was going to join our family," he quickly inserted, his gaze begging Marissa to believe him.

"Oh, but she is."

Another bout of heat scorched Marissa's face, and she was surprised to see Antonio's color deepen as well. Marissa wasn't sure what to say after his grandmother's bold announcement and blurted out the first thing that came to mind. "Why did the roses always have to be yellow? And why only one?"

"Ah, but that is the trait I treasure most in my grandson. His desire to make others happy." Carlotta motioned to the cozy seating arrangement. "Let us sit down, and I will tell you the story of the yellow rose."

Marissa had no choice but to sit beside Antonio on a short couch, not much bigger than a loveseat, since Carlotta took the facing chair. Primly, nervously, Marissa folded her hands and set them atop her knees as she leaned slightly forward. She sensed Antonio fidgeting and was surprised to discover he must be feeling just as awkward.

"After my first performance in *A Rose in the Night*, before it was made into a movie, a young man in an outdated suit came to my dressing room with a single yellow rose in his hand," Carlotta said. "He handed it to me and said, 'You'll always be remembered in my heart, Miss Milano, because you'll always be the rose of my life.' Of course, I was a little stunned and leery of the man, a stranger to me. He was obviously no swank New Yorker, this one, though he was handsome in a rugged sort of way—but clumsy, too. He accidentally stepped on my toe with his big boot that first night, and I threw him out of my dressing room." She chuckled, lost in a time before Marissa or Antonio had been born.

"The second night he came again, and then a third. At first, as I said, he unnerved me with his yellow roses and gentle-mannered words. I had recently been jilted by the man I thought I loved and wanted nothing to do with any male. But after a time I started looking for the man with the rose to come, hoping he would. When he didn't show up at the theater on the eighth night and a messenger brought the rose, I grew worried and made inquiries. I discovered that he'd been hit by a car, though he wasn't seriously injured. But he'd had the presence of mind to remember my flower and made arrangements to send it."

Marissa was entranced by the story and leaned closer.

"I was stunned, intrigued, and I visited him at the hospital," Carlotta continued. "We talked for hours, and romance grew between us. A single rose continued to come each night, and when he was able to walk—his leg was in a cast—he did, too, this time delivering the flower in person. I wondered why he never sent a basket or bouquets like other admirers did, but that's what set his lone rose apart. It stood out, as he did. And yellow was my favorite color—a fact he had unearthed from the stage manager, I later discovered. He sent me a yellow rose each night of my performance and on throughout my short movie career, until I made the decision to quit acting, become a cattleman's wife, and marry him. That man, of course, was my Frederick. And Antonio is much as he was. Each time he visits, he brings me a yellow rose, to remind me of happier times."

She looked with fondness at her grandson, and Marissa was hard-pressed not to cry. Her eyes were watering, and seeing no box of tissues, she used one of her wide sleeves to blot under her eyes.

"My story pleases you?" Carlotta said with a smile. "Come with me, and we will find you a tissue. I want to put my rose in water, and then we will all three share dinner. Yes?"

"Yes," Marissa agreed with a laughing little smile.

Carlotta led the way to her rooms while Marissa walked beside Antonio, feeling a little self-conscious in view of all the recent revelations. The tiny woman opened a brown, carved door at the end of the hall, and Marissa stepped after her into a well-furnished and luxurious apartment. She spotted the 1910 curio cabinet instantly.

Her gaze flew to Antonio, and he gave her a nervous

smile. Carlotta beamed. "Is it not beautiful? My Antonio gave it to me for my eighty-ninth birthday. It reminds me much of my mother's when I was a girl in Spain." She picked up a slender vase nearby and filled it with water from the adjoining minikitchen. With the utmost care she unwrapped the flower from the plastic and propped it in the water. "There, my Frederick. See what a good boy our Antonio is, to remember the love we shared?"

The murmured words again brought tears to Marissa's eyes, and she took a tissue from a nearby box. Before they left Carlotta's small home to accompany her to dinner, Marissa stopped Antonio with her hand to his arm. He turned, and she stood on tiptoe to kiss the smooth spot on his jaw next to his mouth.

"What was that for?" he asked, shock written in his eyes.

"Just for being the most thoughtful man and the best grandson in the whole world." She loved the stunned expression that crossed his face, brushed the frosted pink lipstick from the dark skin near his open mouth with the pad of her thumb, then gave him a happy little smile before leaving the room to follow Carlotta.

◆

Throughout the roast beef dinner, Antonio watched Marissa and his grandmother engage in animated conversation, as if they'd been best friends for life. Even if he had a book as a guide, he probably would never figure women out. His grandmother had been adamant that no one should know her whereabouts. Yet here she was, sitting across from Antonio and lightly scolding him for not bringing Marissa to the center sooner.

And Marissa—she was one of those unsolved mysteries who likely would always remain that way. One minute she was shouting in the parking lot, accusing him of things that made no sense, and not ten minutes later she was kissing him gently, her touch causing his heart to race with hope and leaving him as tongue-tied as a youth on his first date. Then, with a playful smile, she had walked away. Throughout the meal, she'd cast him adoring glances, ones that said he now stood in a class with her cat and lime sherbet and antiques— and everything else Marissa valued.

Antonio cherished these visits with his grandmother as much as she did, but after the umpteenth smiling, dreamy-eyed glance Marissa sent his way, he stood up from the table. It was time to get this thing settled once and for all.

His grandmother looked at him in surprised regret. "You are leaving already?"

"Today, yes. But I promise to make next Saturday's visit longer." He walked around the table and kissed her cheek.

"You're a good boy, Antonio." His grandmother patted his jaw and gripped his chin in a loving manner. She turned to Marissa. "And you will come again to visit me also? Yes?"

"I'd love to," Marissa said, rising from her chair and also coming around the table to bend down and deposit a kiss on his grandmother's other cheek. "I can't take another Saturday off for awhile, but once the wedding season has slackened off, I should be able to come then. And I'll bring that dress book I was telling you about. I think you'll adore looking through the patterns we use. Sometimes we use pictures, too, much like your wedding picture." Marissa's eyes went wide, and she straightened. "The picture! That's what I forgot."

"There is a problem?" Carlotta asked.

The worry instantly left Marissa's eyes, and a smile lifted her lips. "Nothing I can't handle. I just recalled something I forgot to do for one of my clients' weddings. I'll work over-time tonight to see that it's taken care of."

Carlotta took Marissa's hand in hers and patted it. "You

will make my Antonio a good wife. You have my blessing."

Marissa's mouth parted in shock. But it wasn't despair that crossed her face in the brief moment Antonio caught her expression before she bent to pick up her purse. The emotion that lit her eyes had seemed more like hope.

He took hold of Marissa's arm. "*Te quiero, abuelita,*" he said to his grandmother, telling her that he loved her.

"*Y yo te quiero también,*" his grandmother said back. "And drive carefully."

Antonio would have liked to initiate the oncoming conversation with Marissa, but the moment he steered her into the empty corridor, she began firing questions his way.

"Why didn't you tell me about your grandmother? She's so sweet and fun to talk with. And why the big secret that the yellow rose was for her?"

Antonio dredged up every bit of patience he had left as they headed for the outside doors. "She asked me not to tell anyone she was living here. She didn't want the media to find out and exploit her peace or privacy."

"But you could have at least told me the rose was for your grandmother, rather than keeping me totally in the dark," Marissa argued, as he swung the door open for both of them, letting Marissa go first. She waited until he resumed his place beside her. "You didn't have to tell me her name. I just don't understand what all the mystery was about."

"I had fully intended to bring you here to meet her some day in the future. I was afraid that once you started me talking about her I might reveal too much. I idolized my grandmother when I was a boy. After seeing her movies I wanted to be just like her. A great addition to the acting world. She's also a wonderful Christian woman, and it was she who introduced me to the Lord when I was nine."

The smile Marissa beamed his way rivaled the sunshine

that filtered from a mass of gray clouds in the west. Spinning off-track, his mind focused on her beauty, and he almost forgot what he wanted to say. Before she could head for the parking lot, he again grasped her arm.

"Wait. We need to talk." Seeking out a spot, he looked toward the lounge chairs, now empty, near the fountain. "Let's sit over there."

"Okay." She seemed nervous. "So is your grandmother the reason you moved to Wadleyville?" she asked quickly, as though to avoid Antonio's questions before he had a chance to ask them.

"She was a major part of it, yes. When I got her letter, stating she'd sold the farm and moved to a retirement center, I was shocked. No child or grandchild likes to think of his parents as growing too old to function in society. After reading her letter, I decided I wanted to be with her for whatever time she had left. She asked me to visit soon, lightly alluding to some health problems, and I decided to make Ohio my permanent home."

Marissa's features sharpened in concern. "Is she very sick?"

"No, after talking to her doctor, I discovered that any ailments are minor, and he expects her to live to see a hundred." Antonio grinned. "The retirement center was a pleasant surprise, too. She has many friends, stays active, and is anything but nonfunctional. She even heads up the entertainment committee, though, of course, most everyone here knows her as Carlotta Porter."

"I'm glad she's happy. She's a very nice lady."

"She is that. Now"—Antonio sobered as he took a seat in the chair facing hers—"would you please explain to me what diabolical deed you thought I had in mind when you confronted me in the parking lot earlier?"

❧

Marissa would rather crawl into a hole somewhere than answer his question. She squirmed, leaning forward to put her hands between her knees, and studied the scuffed toes of her loafers. She made a mental note to buy a bottle of bone-colored polish after work tonight. A sudden forgotten piece of information soared through her brain, giving her words flight as she jerked her head upward.

"Maybe the yellow rose has been explained, but what about the phone call?"

"Phone call?"

Marissa took a quick breath, hoping she was doing the right thing by bringing it up. "The one you made at the shop last night. You said something about not wanting to do some woman in." She swallowed. "You seemed very angry with whoever it was you were talking to."

His furrowed brows smoothed out, and his face cleared. "You must mean my car! I was talking to the man at the garage. He hadn't returned my calls all day, and I was upset about that, as well as about the news he gave me."

"Your car?" Marissa squeaked.

Antonio nodded in resignation. "She got me all the way from California and has been with me for more than five years, but Ed couldn't get the part he needed. He tried everywhere—they don't make it anymore—and he suggested that she wasn't worth more trouble and I junk her. It was a hard decision to make. She was such a sweet old girl."

"Your car," Marissa repeated in disbelief.

Antonio frowned. "It just occurred to me that you thought I was a killer?" He phrased the statement as a question.

"Well, not originally." Marissa gulped down the bitter taste of foolishness, and her next words came out sheepishly. "At first I thought you might be a cat burglar."

Antonio's eyes widened, and Marissa, feeling the need to reveal that she had at least a grain of intelligence, hastened to explain, "It all made sense at the time. His calling card is a yellow rose—and that's all you ever wanted. Every Saturday, which is when he also strikes."

"You thought I was the cat burglar?" Suddenly Antonio laughed, a disbelieving chuckle that turned into an all-out gut-wrenching belly laugh.

Marissa grabbed her purse, stood, and stomped toward her car. She didn't need this! She already knew she was a nominee for the Stupidest Person on the Planet Award and didn't need him to remind her.

"Marissa," he gasped at the end of another chuckle. "Wait!"

She kept walking. Behind her his chair legs scraped the patio, and the gritty crunch of his footsteps grew louder. Soon his hand touched her arm. "I'm sorry I laughed. Let me explain."

She pivoted and glared at him. "Yes?"

His lips twitched, and she just prevented herself from hitting him on the arm with her purse. "When I first met you, I wondered the same thing about you—if you were the cat burglar. I found you scrounging around in my bushes, and then I read an article in the newspaper about the theft. You always seemed to be following me, and I knew you liked antique jewelry."

"You thought *I* was the cat burglar?" she whispered, her expression stunned.

"Only at first—I wondered about it. But I figured you either had to be a thief with very poor judgment to pick me as a target, or I was completely off-base." He grinned. "I do have an old high school ring with an emerald in it, and my grandfather's antique gold pocket watch and his ring, but other than those few heirlooms, my luxuries are few."

She smiled then giggled, finally seeing the absurdity of the situation. They had each suspected the other one!

Antonio joined in her chuckles, and her laughter grew so

great that she doubled over, holding onto his arm for support. When she could finally wipe the tears from her eyes, she noticed they again had an audience, a well-dressed couple out for an evening stroll. The slender, white-haired gentleman nodded their way and smiled then turned back to the plump lady on his arm. Marissa realized how late it was and looked at her watch.

"Oh, no. I have to get back to the shop."

"Before you go, I'd like to bring up another subject, one my grandmother mentioned."

Marissa looked up. "Okay."

"I never told her I intended to marry you. But she can read me well and probably figured it out from the talks we've had." Marissa's face grew rosy, but Antonio went on. "She has a bold way of speaking things straight out, but she's right. I do want our relationship to progress to another level."

"No more friends only?" she asked softly.

"No more friends only."

She smiled. "Okay."

Antonio blinked. He had expected more reluctance on her part, or at least some hesitation, and had been prepared to plead his case. Would he ever figure this woman out?

"I want to learn to trust again, after what happened with Grant," she explained. "So please bear with me. Trust is forgotten territory right now, and I'm taking it one step at a time. But I do like you, Antonio. That's what made this whole cat-burglar thing hard to deal with. The fact that I like you."

His expression softened, and he took both her hands in his. "I'll give you all the time you need, Rissa." He bent his head to kiss her. A sweet, reassuring, warm kiss that made her tingle all over. "Only know," he said as he pulled away, "that when we're together, I see no one but you."

"I guess that's not too surprising since I sometimes wear

sugar mustaches and the beginnings of blue-ink beards."

"At least now I have the right to kiss them off." He chuckled.

Heat colored her face. "The ink, too?"

He seemed to consider. "No, for that I'll keep my bandana handy." He winked, and she grinned. "How about we seal our new arrangement with a lime sherbet—and then you can see what else I do on Saturday nights? I should warn you though; you might want to follow me in your car. I usually don't get home 'til after midnight. I often run errands afterward or spend time with Joe."

"Sounds intriguing, and I wish I could, but I have to get back to the shop." She quirked a brow. "But I'd still be very interested in knowing what else it is you do on Saturdays. And who Joe is. It vill be nice not to have to resort to ze water torture method to get ze information from you," she added in a horrible German accent.

He laughed at her silliness. "You're too kind, Fräulein. I teach drama classes at a youth center in a slum district near Columbus. The pay is minimal, but the benefits of helping troubled kids find an outlet for their bottled-up anger is worth it."

She looked at him with surprise. "How did all this come about?"

"The other reason I came to Ohio. Joe, a friend, wrote me a month before I received my grandmother's letter, asking me if I'd be interested in the job. He knew I had grandparents here and also knew my history since we grew up together in L.A. I could've ended up being one of those disturbed kids and almost did join a gang at one point, after my mother died."

Marissa's respect for him grew by the minute. "You know, Antonio, I really think you should follow that dream of yours. Maybe God orchestrated all these events in your life—you coming to Wadleyville, becoming a youth drama director, and helping in the Easter play—so that you'd come to the point of wanting to fulfill the plan He has for you. His desires become your desires—as I once told you—and He'll work it all out."

" 'With God all things are possible'?" he asked with a grin, quoting her bumper sticker.

"Yes. But it's not only our state motto. It's a promise to live by."

"You know, it's funny you should bring it up, but at Mike's urging I talked to his uncle in Cincinnati this morning. And he's interested in helping to provide funds for a drama school I hope to open next fall. One that teaches Christian-based drama. Mike's wife is going to write the plays."

Her mouth dropped open. "Antonio! That's wonderful! I'm so happy for you." She threw her arms around his neck in an exuberant hug, thrilled he was following his dream.

"I truly believe this is what God called you to do," she said when she pulled away. "You're so talented at directing. And I really wish I could go with you and see you in action." She dropped her hands from around his neck. "But if I don't get to the shop soon, I'll be there all night. I still have to run by the church where a wedding is scheduled for tomorrow and set up some things. As it is, I'll probably get home after midnight, even if I leave this minute."

"Okay. I'll let you go this time, but only if you promise to come with me three weeks from now, on a night of your choosing, to see my kids perform *West Side Story*."

Her smile was wide. "I wouldn't miss it for the world!"

With another parting kiss and a gentle squeeze of her hands, he let her go. "I'll see you at church."

"I'll save you a place!" She gave a little wave as she hurried to her car, her step as buoyant as her heart. Hearing Carlotta's story and knowing that she, too, had experienced a bad relationship with a former fiancé—but had found a lasting love with Frederick—sparked Marissa's hope that she could find the same with Antonio.

The rest of the day sped by in a haze of planning, setting up, and fixing her error. The young Miss Reynolds had been so worried that something might happen to her great-grandmother's photo, so months ago, after the initial appointment, Marissa had put the snapshot in a protective waterproof folder, which she had then slipped into her file cabinet.

Unfortunately, when she sent the monthly orders to the seamstress, Mrs. Hargrove, she'd forgotten to include the picture since it wasn't in its usual folder. Not all her clients bought their wedding gowns from Marissa's shop, and she hadn't thought anything about the blank lines where the pattern number should be when she'd skimmed through the Reynolds folder. Even Miss Reynolds's measurements had been jotted on a separate paper and put in the envelope with the picture. During that time Marissa's mind had been in a tailspin regarding her suspicions about Antonio, and unfortunately she'd been careless in her work. First with the error in not ordering the right amount of roses for the prom, and now this. It was cutting it close, but there was still enough time for the gown to be made for the wedding next year.

Once she readied the Reynolds correspondence, with a note to return the photograph after it was no longer needed, and put the sealed envelope in her purse to mail, Marissa sat back exhausted. Mrs. Hargrove didn't have a computer so couldn't be easily contacted with the information, and Marissa mentally thanked the Lord for her father. The computer had sped up her work dramatically, putting her in touch with people she'd formerly only corresponded with through regular mail or phone calls, some of them long distance. If she'd known how easy it was to use one, she might have taken computer classes at high school instead of shying away from anything electronic. Now she was seriously considering buying a scanner, which could cut even more time from her workload.

Feeling a headache coming on, the stress of the day catching up with her, Marissa decided to close up shop early and go home. Everything else could wait.

As she drove to the post office to slip the envelope in an outside box, she thought she saw Antonio's blue rental whizzing past in the other direction. She studied her rearview mirror, but he was too far away to tell.

That was odd. Didn't he say he usually got home late on Saturday nights? It was only an hour after sunset.

Marissa decided to pick up a carton of milk along with the needed shoe polish and stopped at a convenience store that sold both. As she drove home, a pearl-like, glowing moon peeked from the edge of thick gray clouds, and she smiled up at it. Her life was finally going right, things were falling into place, and she was in love. Could a day turn out any better?

She turned onto her dead-end street lit by the lonely lamp and thought she saw movement near her home. She slowed the car, curious. Turning off her headlights made it easier to see into the front yards. She rolled along the curbside, wondering why she felt such sharp prickles of unease jump behind her neck.

There! On the second-story side of her house. Was that a filmy curtain liner blowing out the window? She set the brake and turned the motor off. Easing out of her car, she let the door close softly without shutting it all the way and moved closer to investigate.

Her bubble of joy burst as she glanced at the dormer window—open now, though she knew she'd shut and locked it. Dread put her in a stranglehold as a black-panted leg stepped through the open window of her bedroom, followed by a trim, muscled form in a black turtleneck and matching ski mask.

twelve

Oh, no, Antonio. No, no, no.

Marissa's earlier comment to him about her coming home late revisited her. He must be taking advantage of her absence to rob her—maybe because he now knew she suspected him? And then what? Would he leave Wadleyville for another small town, knowing his days were numbered here?

Oddly Marissa felt no anger or even fear. Only sad remorse. She didn't understand why Antonio lied to her, though now that she thought about it, he never denied being the cat burglar. Instead he'd easily switched the topic to his thinking she was the thief.

Oh, clever, clever man. Oh, poor, misguided man.

Was he so trapped by his chains of bondage that he couldn't break free from this life of crime he'd chosen? Maybe—as a kleptomaniac reflexively stole for the sole purpose of stealing and not for the object itself, or as a drug addict mindlessly induced dangerous drugs to obey the demands of a chemically infested body—maybe Antonio took things from others for a similar purpose. Not because he wanted to steal any longer, but because he didn't know how to stop. Because he was addicted to the thrill, the danger. He needed professional help. Could Marissa get him to admit he had a problem and seek that help?

Her love for him hadn't died or even waned, despite seeing that her earlier assumptions of him were correct. Perhaps she was the only one who could get him to listen to reason, since he claimed he loved her, too.

Silently, so as not to make a hint of noise and alert any neighbors who might still be awake, she walked through the grass, avoiding the noisy crunch of the gravel drive, and stopped beneath her bedroom window.

"Antonio," she softly called up to him.

He jumped and almost lost his footing on the roof, grabbing the sill of the still-open window. Marissa's heart settled back into her chest at his near fall, and she could well imagine his expression of surprise that must be under that mask. His head turned sharply in her direction.

"We need to talk," she whispered loudly.

He hesitated then took a few hasty steps along the sloped roof and reached for the thick branch of a nearby oak, swinging into it with Tarzan-like effortlessness, obviously intending to run from her. Evidently he didn't plan to talk to her either. Well, that was fine. She would do all the talking.

"Listen to me," Marissa said a little more loudly, her determination growing stronger by the second. She marched to the tree where he now hung from one branch, ready to drop down in front of her.

"I don't know why you've chosen this lifestyle, but you know it's wrong. I don't have to tell you that."

He dropped to the ground in a crouch and stared at her. Through the holes in the mask, she could see the whites of his eyes as they darted back and forth, scoping out the area.

She lifted her hands in supplication. "If you'll just give this over to Jesus, He'll help you to stop, but only if you let Him. He's our deliverer, and He can deliver you from this awful crime-habit."

Quick as a wink he darted away. Marissa moved just as fast and clamped a hand onto the small black leather satchel that flapped like a woman's shoulder bag from his arm. He twisted and strained to pull it from her, but she held fast with both hands during their tug-of-war fight for the bag. The strap snapped. The satchel fell from her hands. Rubies, sapphires and diamonds spilled onto the grass, caught by a neighbor's porch light nearby.

He fell to his knees and began to scoop them up. She dropped to her knees and grabbed his black-gloved wrists.

"Please, Antonio. Listen to me! I love you. I'm not sure when it happened, but it did. Don't do this to yourself. To us! Let God help you fight this thing. He loves you, too."

He snatched his hands away from her grasp and rocketed to his feet. Leaving the rest of the jewels behind, he raced across the street, for his house.

"Don't run from me!" Marissa chased after him. Her long-ago years as a tomboy in a neighborhood of boys revisited her, and when he hit the grass she leaped out, arms outstretched, and tackled him. They both fell to the ground, panting for breath.

Football hadn't been the only sport she'd played, and before he could recover and collect his thoughts, she grabbed his arm and pulled it up behind him, though this time she didn't make him say "uncle" as she had to the boys who teased her about her freckles and knobby knees when she was nine.

"Stop struggling to get away and listen to me!" Marissa whispered urgently as she straddled his back. "Are you listening to me?"

"Yes," he groaned in a high-pitched, pain-filled voice.

"Good. I once knew some kids in high school who had the same problem, though they never took it to the level you have. But they thought stealing was cool. One ended up in prison, which isn't cool at all. The other boy sought help. Our pastor counseled with him for weeks. He got off on parole and cleaned up his act, and now he works in a prison ministry. He even visited the first guy I told you about—who's in prison a second time for armed robbery." She leaned closer to speak low into his mask-covered ear. "So which side of the bars do you want to be on? The inside or the outside?"

He didn't answer, and she drove her point home. "I know it was hard for you, not having a father. Having a mother who worked all the time and pushed you to succeed. Never having much of a childhood and feeling the need to be a man and support your family before you were ready—but this isn't the way to get riches. The Bible even says we're not to store up for ourselves treasures the moth corrupts, or ones that get broken or old or stolen—okay, those are my words, but it's what that verse means. We're supposed to store up for ourselves treasures in heaven that never diminish. And we do that by obeying God and being righteous—something we can only be when we accept His Son Jesus and are washed clean in the blood He shed for us."

Marissa paused to gulp down a breath. "But you know all that already. You've been to church and heard the message. Still, even now, if you repent and ask God to help you and forgive you—He will. And I'll stand with you through it all, no matter what happens. I promise."

He jerked as though in surprise then lay still for a few seconds, and she relaxed her hold on his arm. Suddenly, as though a bolt of energy zapped him, he whipped his other hand to the ground, out of her grasp, arched his back, and threw her off like a bucking bronco does its rider.

"Oh!" She landed with a rustled thump in the grass.

He struggled to his feet, bypassed his front door, and took off running in the direction of the woods.

"Oh, Antonio," she muttered sadly under her breath. "I won't let you ruin your life. Not if I can help it!"

Jumping to her feet, she raced after him.

❧

Planning to settle in front of the TV with his nighttime snack of barbecue-flavored curly fries, Antonio took a seat on the black vinyl couch he'd bought cheap at a yard sale last month. He was glad he'd made the decision to let Christ take control of his finances and his life, and now he wished he hadn't waited so long to make that choice. Already it felt as if a burden had been bulldozed off him. He wasn't naive and knew that starting an acting school would take a great deal of his time and a major commitment, as well as a good part of his own savings. Yet he trusted this decision was from God. He would work it all out somehow.

Seeing a shadow dart by his window, Antonio threw the sack aside and jumped up to investigate. His eyes widened when he saw Marissa, clad in her black pantsuit, her light hair streaming behind her as she ran. That was weird. From this angle he spotted her car parked three houses up the street. What was she doing over at his house, this late, when he'd already told her he wouldn't be home? Looking for her cat again? And why had she parked in such an odd location and not in her own driveway?

Cat burglar whispered through his mind, but he didn't want to believe it. Not of her, the woman he'd grown to love and hoped someday to marry. No. Not Marissa.

Still, he had told her about his grandfather's gold pocket watch. Once, when he was a teenager, he pawned it. When his aunt found out, she hit the roof, giving Antonio a tongue-lashing he never forgot. Somehow she got it back—probably threatening the pawnbroker with bodily harm if he didn't release it to her—and only before she left for Spain had she entrusted it to Antonio again. He never let go of it. Nor the gold ring that had been his grandfather's.

Was Marissa a thief, planning to steal his small cache of valuables? His heart argued the point, but his logical mind couldn't come up with a solid reason for her parking her car in a place other than her own driveway. She'd known he hadn't planned to come home until later tonight. If practice hadn't ended early because of a phoned-in bomb threat, one he was thankful turned out to be a hoax, he would still be there. He peered harder at her vehicle, seen in a neighbor's porch light. Yes, it was her car, all right. He looked at her dark house and could just make out Sherlock sitting in the dining room window.

So she wasn't after her cat this time.

A loud rustle of bushes and a thump hit the side of his house, nearest the woods. Only seconds had elapsed since Antonio first saw her through the window. He had to put a stop to this. Dreading what he must do, he hurried out the front door, not even bothering to slip his shoes on. He had to talk some sense into her before she threw her life away.

"Will you please listen to me?" she furiously whispered from the other side of the house. "Why won't you talk to me?"

Antonio froze. She had a partner? He heard a grunt, a loud rustle as though someone fell, then footsteps running through the grass. He turned the corner in time to spot Marissa scrambling to a stand and heading for the woods. Speeding after her, he easily caught her, throwing his arms around her middle. She gave a surprised shriek and began to struggle, kicking backward and hitting his arms with her fists like a crazed little wildcat.

"Let me go!" she screamed.

"Marissa!" he yelled. "Stop it!"

She halted in mid-kick-punch-swing and turned her head to look over her shoulder. Her eyes were saucer-wide. Her mouth dropped open.

"Antonio?"

"Who else?" he said grimly and released her.

She pivoted to face him. Her features were a mask of strained white as she darted a glance toward the trees. "Cat burglar," she whispered.

Antonio looked to see a dark-clothed figure dash into the woods. Shock momentarily knocked him speechless then he took off running after him. "Stay there!" he called back to Marissa. "No—call the police!"

❧

Once Marissa phoned the police from Antonio's house, the shock that she'd grappled with a real cat burglar—a stranger and not Antonio—began to fade, and she stopped shaking so much. She went outside to wait, her worried gaze frequently going to the trees. Was Antonio all right? Had the thief hurt him?

Finally she couldn't stand it any longer. She went inside to retrieve the flashlight she'd seen on the kitchen counter and jogged toward the woods. The real burglar had ample opportunity to hurt Marissa while trying to get away and never did, except to push her down. So obviously his standards went above hitting women. She relied on that bit of knowledge as she reached the edge of the woods.

At the wail of sirens she hesitated, soon seeing red and blue lights crazily flash across the neighborhood like colored strobes. Two police cars squealed to a stop at the dead-end street, and uniformed men instantly exited their cars.

"The burglar's this way!" Marissa yelled, turning on her light and directing the white beam toward the path. She took off running through the gap in the trees before they could detain her and make her stay behind.

She slowed to a jog, but in the crazy bouncing beam of her flashlight she couldn't see much to guide her. Stiff twigs scraped her exposed skin. Tiny sharp rocks found their way into her loafers. Still she ran-slid-stumbled along the main path.

"Antonio!" she called. "Where are you?"

She stopped to catch her breath, clutched her knees, and strained her ears for any noise that would direct her to the men. Off another dirt trail she heard the sound of bushes rustle then grunting and dull smacks—the unmistakable sound of men fighting.

Marissa took off in that direction, never stopping to consider that she might be putting herself in danger. She'd been unfair to Antonio, judging him wrongly, and she owed him whatever help she could give in bringing in the real thief. After all, if she hadn't intervened and tried to stop the burglar, Antonio wouldn't even be in this predicament.

She came to the clearing with the waterfall. Her light picked up a form lying on the ground, struggling to get up. The gray T-shirt and blue jeans made it obvious who the man was.

"Antonio!" Marissa fell to her knees beside him. His nose was bloody, and he had a bruise on one cheek. She put a gentle hand to his face.

"I thought I told you to stay at the house," he grumbled, in obvious pain.

Hearing splashing, she looked up and directed the flashlight that way. The thief was limp-running across the shallow stream.

"Oh, no, you don't!" Marissa cried. She rocketed up, dropped the flashlight, and went after him.

"Marissa!" Antonio yelled. "Come back!"

Ignoring him, she high-stepped it through the water as fast as she could. Before the burglar could hobble to the bank, she tackled him around his middle, and they both fell with a loud splash.

"Let meeb globe," he burbled in the water.

"Nothin' doin'," Marissa said, though she moved her weight further down his back so he could raise his shoulders above water and not drown. "I don't especially feel like chasing you through these woods all night." She turned her head and shouted. "Officers! We're over here—in the stream! I have the thief!"

The man attempted to get away, thrashing his arms to get a hold on the slippery rock, but she held on fast this time.

She heard more splashing, and soon Antonio was beside her in the water, with the flashlight. "You don't listen very well, do you?" he asked, frustration mixed with admiration in his voice. "Where'd you learn to tackle like that?"

"Before puberty I was the most-feared tomboy in Wadleyville," she said with a grin. "I grew out of it though."

The look on his face said otherwise. "Just remind me never to make you mad." His voice was teasing. "You never cease to amaze me. I never know what's coming next."

"Hey, remember me?" the burglar asked bitterly. "You planning to press me flat like a pancake, or will you let me breathe now?"

Marissa felt like giving a little sitting jump on his back for the offhanded remark about her few-pounds-over-the-limit weight but gritted her teeth instead and gripped his shirt in a tighter clutch. "Officers! I got him!" she yelled again, hearing rustling nearby and seeing bright spots from their flashlights through the thick undergrowth.

"So let's see who's been causing all the excitement," Antonio muttered and pulled off the ski mask. He shone the light into the man's face.

The burglar cursed. "Get that thing out of my eyes!"

Marissa almost toppled off her prisoner. Though she could see only his profile and the wet clumps of hair on his white face, she recognized the onyx cross earring the man wore. "You were at the auction!" she exclaimed. "Standing next to that woman in the black hat. And I've seen you at other auctions before that."

"Go to the head of the class," the man muttered.

"He must've somehow gotten the addresses of those who won items at the auctions from the auctioneer's record books," she said to Antonio, her voice filled with the excitement of discovery. "He probably heard that woman and me discussing our jewelry and targeted us as likely victims. Her home was burglarized, too, you know."

Running steps and splashes filled the next few moments as the police converged upon them. Antonio helped Marissa off the half-drowned burglar, and two officers pulled him to his feet. One slapped him in handcuffs; another read him his rights. A third officer kept his flashlight's beam on the thief.

All the while the young man stared at an equally drenched Marissa, an odd mixture of anger, disgust, and frank curiosity in his one blue eye that wasn't swollen and blackened. Light red hairs in the beginning of a beard covered the jaw of his lean face, and his wet-darkened hair hung in clumps around his neck. Before they took him away, he stood his ground.

"I just have one question for the lady." His words were mocking but seemed urgent, too.

"Come on." A policeman pulled on his shackled arm. "You don't need to be disturbing these decent folks any longer."

"No," Marissa stepped forward, feeling Antonio's reassuring presence beside her. She tucked the wet chunk of her hair that stuck to her cheek behind one ear. "It's okay. Let him ask."

The officer relaxed his hold and nodded.

"Before, when you thought I was that guy Antonio, and you told me you loved me and stuff, I thought you were nuts."

Marissa swallowed, feeling Antonio's sharp gaze swing her way at the untimely revelation of her feelings for him.

"But later," the man continued, "when you tackled me that first time, you started saying things there's no way you could've known. Like how my father left us when I was a kid and I had to take care of my family, and all that other stuff. How'd you know about that? And how'd you know my real name? We were never introduced. But even if we had been, everyone only knows me by my nickname."

"What?" Chill bumps having nothing to do with the breeze or her drenched condition broke out along Marissa's arms.

"You called me by name. You said, 'Even now, if you repent and ask God to help you and forgive you, Dominick— He will.'"

Marissa just stared, slowly shaking her head back and forth. She'd never known his name—given or otherwise. She thought she'd been addressing Antonio the entire time. Had the young man just imagined she'd said his name, or. . .

An other-worldly shiver coursed through her being as she met Antonio's surprised gaze.

Had the Holy Spirit taken her words and sent His own message to Dominick's heart?

"God knew your name, Dominick," she said softly. "He was the one who called you. Not me."

Dominick stared at her a few seconds, a look close to fear in his one open blue eye. Then any such emotion disappeared, and with a cocky nod at the officer holding him he said, "I'm ready now. It sure took you guys long enough. I thought she was either going to drown me or squash me to death."

Marissa thoughtfully watched them walk away. In her spirit she felt the Lord tell her what to do, and she stepped forward. "Excuse me, Officer?"

The uniformed man closest to her stopped.

She watched Dominick's retreating form limp between the two policemen as they took him away to a waiting car; then she looked at the husky man in front of her.

"I'd like to visit him in jail, if it's at all possible."

The man scratched the back of his neck. "Well, I don't see why not. Incidentally"—he pulled something from his pocket—"this yours?"

Marissa looked at the shimmering diamond necklace in his hand and nodded.

"We found it on him. We'll have to keep it for evidence, of course."

"Of course. Keep it as long as you need to."

"We'll also need to investigate the crime scene and ask you some questions," he said. "Though I suppose the questioning can wait 'til the morning if you're too tired tonight."

"Yes, thank you. But, please, feel free to look through my house. It's the yellow one with the white trim—oh, but whatever you do, don't let the cat out! Maybe I should come with you."

"No hurry, Miss. Go ahead and take a few minutes to catch a breather." He looked at Antonio as he spoke then smiled at both of them. "I'm sure glad this case is finally on its way to being solved. You'll get the reward money, of course, but just between us I'm hoping to get a promotion."

"Reward money?" Marissa repeated.

"Yeah. Fifty thousand dollars."

"Fifty *thou-sand*—?" If Antonio hadn't come up behind her, Marissa would've fallen over.

"Just one piece of advice, Miss. Next time let the police handle it. You did all right, but if he'd been armed you could've gotten hurt worse than your friend here." The policeman tipped his hat and moved to join his fellow officers.

Feeling duly chastised, Marissa numbly followed. Antonio's hand on her arm stopped her. "Just a minute," he said, his voice firm. "Don't you have something you want to tell me?"

Marissa gulped. In the single white beam from the flashlight now sitting on a waist-high boulder, tilted at a crazy angle on their torsos, she had enough light to see that he'd wiped the blood from his nose; but the bruise under his eye looked painful. "I'm sorry I got you into this."

"That's not what I was talking about."

"We'll split the reward money, of course. After the tithe I'll use my half toward my wedding chapel, and your half I'm sure you'll want to use for the drama school. Can you believe it, Antonio? Our dreams will be coming true faster than we'd ever imagined!"

"You're right. It is an answer to prayer, but I wasn't talking about the reward money either."

"No?" She swallowed, feeling a little dizzy by the serious I'm-not-letting-you-get-away-this-time note in his voice. She could imagine the intensity of his eyes as they stared at her and was glad the flashlight's beam didn't carry high enough to pick that up.

"I'm talking about what Dominick said earlier. What you told him."

"Isn't that amazing? I never even knew his name, but God must've been calling out to him. I still have goose bumps after hearing what he said."

"Yes, it is amazing, but that's still not what I was talking about. You said it to a stranger when you thought he was me. Can't you say it one more time?"

Hearing the thread of pleading in his voice, she gave up. "You mean the part about me loving you?"

In the scant light she could see his lips turn up at the corners. "Yes, that's the part I meant. But did *you* mean it?"

"Yes," she admitted, preparing also to tell him how sorry she was for suspecting him a second time.

Before she could apologize, he captured her lips with his. His kiss was at first sweet and gentle, then longer, the kiss of a man who realized that something bad could have happened to either of them—but by God's grace it hadn't. Marissa's emotions felt tossed about but strangely soothed, too, as if her chilled body had been doused in warm oil.

He pulled away but kept his arms locked around her.

She giggled. "I'm all wet—and I've made you even wetter."

"I don't mind. But I guess we should be getting back. After we both get some dry clothes on and the police leave, we obviously need to talk, long and hard, and clear up a lot of things. First of all, before we go any further, I am *not* a thief. I stole a box of Cracker Jacks when I was seven—but I got my hide tanned good, and I've never stolen again. I didn't get the box either."

"Cracker Jacks?" Marissa asked with an amused giggle.

"I wanted the spy decoder ring inside."

"Ah, so then you had aspirations of joining the war on crime and becoming a secret agent?"

"Every small boy does." He dropped one arm from around her waist, picked up the flashlight, and began to walk back with her to the main path. Suddenly he stopped and turned his head her way. "No more playing detective, okay? This is the end of your career."

"Oh, all right," she said with mock grudging in her voice though she was touched by the concern she heard in his. "I suppose you'll just have to feed my detecting yearnings by watching old mystery flicks with me and helping me solve those kinds of cases."

"Marissa"—his voice was now teasing—"no offense. But you make one lousy detective—though you're not half bad as a linebacker." He grabbed her hands before she could playfully hit his chest. "Still, I love you just the way you are. Sugar mustaches, blue-ink beards, and all the other little surprises included."

He kissed her again, sending her heart into orbit. Marissa hoped this was only the start of a mutually satisfying relationship between them. After all, who else but a former actor could appreciate her crazy stunts? And, as far as Antonio went, Marissa could think of a lot of things to appreciate about him!

epilogue

Marissa sat at the cherry-wood dresser of the cruise liner's luxury cabin and unfastened the necklace with the gold rose charm that Antonio had bought her for a wedding present. Carefully she set the fragile chain in her travel jewelry box then picked up the velvet case with the antique diamond choker inside. She had brought all her jewels from home for this cruise. It was the perfect place to wear them. She circled the glistening gems around her neck, but with her long nails she couldn't fasten the clasp.

"Hon," she muttered. "Could you help me a second?"

Antonio stopped scrambling around in his open suitcase, which lay on a queen-sized cobalt blue bedspread that matched the floor-length curtains and carpet. The colors provided a refreshing visual of the ocean extending into their comfortable cabin. Cream accents and cherry-wood furniture completed the tasteful decor.

"Sure." He came up behind her and grabbed each end of the diamond choker around her neck, working to fasten it. In the dresser mirror Marissa saw midway up his pinky finger the plastic spy decoder ring she'd given him as a giggle-gift yesterday in the taxi on the way to the ship and their honeymoon cruise. She had found the ring at an estate sale weeks ago, in a box of forgotten items the harried woman of the house didn't even remember.

"You're not actually going to wear that ring to dinner, are you?" Marissa quirked an eyebrow.

"No?" Antonio questioned her as if he'd thought about it.

"I think you like that silly gift better than the real gift of the engraved box I gave you." Her words were said in mock dismay, though she couldn't keep the amused light out of her eyes.

"Not so," Antonio replied. "And I love the message you had inscribed on the gold plate: 'Forever, with all my love and trust. Marissa.' It'll be perfect for Grandfather's watch and ring." He finished fastening the necklace, gave her neck a loving nuzzle, then straightened, his hands still on her shoulders.

She smiled back at him in the mirror. Trust had been a hard issue for her to come by, but with time and the Lord's help she had learned to trust a man again. This man.

When Grant betrayed her, the thief of insecurity had taken her unawares and stolen her joy and trust, leaving behind for Marissa his destructive calling card of jealousy and suspicion. Through these past two years God had restored to her joy, peace, and love—and she'd mentally torn up the thief's long-ago calling card and thrown it back in his face. Of course, she knew better than to believe everyone who came along. But toward Antonio, who'd been so patient and kind as she worked through her problems, she felt loving and absolute trust.

"I can't find my shaving kit, though I know I packed it." He turned back to his search.

"Oh, but I kind of like you with that dark shadow on your jaw. Must you shave it off?"

"For a formal dinner, yes. Next time I'll leave it on just for you." He burrowed deeper into his bag. "Can you believe it took the Jensens up until dessert last night to convince them I wasn't *that* Antonio? I don't want to draw even more attention to myself."

Marissa giggled and took a moment to eye him in the mirror. He really was drop-dead gorgeous, and while he did favor the actor she'd always been able to see the differences, too.

A congratulatory bouquet of gaily colored daisies and carnations among feathery greens from Dominick caught her eye. An arrangement he'd asked their pastor to order for him from the new florist shop's owner—Linda's cousin. Both Marissa and Antonio now visited Dominick in prison twice a month, ever since he'd been sentenced for the burglaries. When they first went to see him in jail, a few days after he'd been caught, he'd been angrily mocking. But that hadn't deterred Marissa from what she felt the Lord telling her to do. Over time, when the visits to him became standard, Dominick grew hesitantly curious then openly receptive, even treating their pastor with respect when he also came. He'd asked a lot of questions concerning the Bible and God, and Marissa was thrilled when two months ago during a visit Dominick asked her and Antonio to lead him in a prayer to accept Jesus Christ as his Lord.

The plea bargaining had won Dominick a reduced sentence, and upon his release in a year he agreed to Antonio's job offer as an assistant at his new drama school. Marissa just hoped Leah, who was now taking classes at Heaven's Door Acting Academy as its first scholarship student, wasn't drawn to Dominick. The young man was a looker, but at present a danger to easily influenced teenage girls who were mad at the world. Leah hadn't been at all happy to learn of Antonio's marriage, and Marissa knew the girl nurtured a full-blown crush on him. Dominick was now a Christian, but a baby one who needed to be fed the Word so he could grow and learn to say no to sin. Marissa would just have to pray especially hard for both of them. Given time, God could work it all out. After all, He'd worked out her life quite well.

Antonio came to her side and bent near her ear. "Get ready," he whispered then kissed her temple and headed for the bathroom, his shaving kit now in hand.

Smiling, Marissa twirled up strands of her hair, fastening them with glittering combs that matched the pine-green embroidery on the bodice and sleeves of her ankle-length, mist-green gown. A hint of perfume, a brush of lip gloss, and she was ready. She moved toward the large square-shaped cabin window and studied the ever-changing beauty of the Atlantic Ocean as the sun began to sink below the horizon, gilding the never-ending water with a gold and crimson sheen.

The opening music of a show on the television set hanging from a corner of the ceiling caught her attention. Recognizing the hour-long drama, she picked up the nearby remote and turned up the volume. Entranced, she watched an unfolding real-life case story. Her eyes widened, and her heart pounded with recognition.

The door to the bathroom opened. "Are you ready?" He let out a whistle. "You are one gorgeous woman."

"Antonio," she breathed, his compliment barely noticed. "Look!" She turned from the set for a second to make sure he was watching, noticed how handsome he looked in his black tux and tie, then turned back to an old newsreel of one of America's most wanted—a man the FBI was searching for.

"See that woman in the crowd behind him?" she asked. "The tall, dark-headed one? I think I've seen her before! Last night at the captain's table—she's on this ship! I can't believe it. Now that I think about it, she was unusually quiet and mysterious. She hardly spoke a word all through dinner. I'll bet she's that wanted man's accomplice and they have something planned at one of the Mediterranean ports—he might be on this ship, too! Maybe I should tell the captain so he can look into it and inform the police—"

In several long strides Antonio was beside her. Grabbing her shoulders, he turned her around to face him—then kissed her firmly on the mouth. Her initial light struggles to get him to understand were forgotten as the kiss grew longer.

When he lifted his head, she blinked her eyes open and tried to get her bearings. "Wow—where did that come from?" She kept her arms tightly fastened around his neck.

He grinned, but she could see desire's flame glowing in his eyes. "At the wedding reception Judy told me that if you started to go off on one of your mystery-P.I. tangents, this might be the best way to get your mind off it and back to other things."

Marissa felt the blush. Her matron of honor knew how deeply she'd fallen in love with this man. The method had been disturbingly effective. Still—

Antonio must have sensed the U-turn her mind had taken for he laid his index finger against her lips before she could argue her case. "Sweetheart, I love you, but as a detective you'll never make it. That 'dark-headed mystery woman' is the captain's mother. From what I heard she's lived in Tennessee all her life, and this is her first trip anywhere— probably why she's so quiet. I seriously doubt she's that mafia guy's accomplice."

"No, I guess not," Marissa agreed, now feeling silly.

"Maybe you should help Sandy write the stories my drama classes perform," he teased.

"Me write a story?" With a little roll of her eyes she gave him a smirk. "I'll just stick to running my wedding chapel and being your wife, thanks. Anyway, you're right about one thing. I do make a lousy detective."

"But a great companion. The best a man could ever have."

She grinned, running her fingers along his now-smooth jaw. "I like it this way, too."

His smile matched hers. "Before we go to dinner, I want you to stand right there and close your eyes."

Puzzled, she looked at him. "Why?"

"Just humor me, please."

Marissa did so, smiling. He stepped away from her, and she heard him turn off the TV then move over the carpet to the small refrigerator in their cabin. The rustle of tissue paper met her ears as he rejoined her.

"Okay, you can open them now."

When she did, Marissa saw that he held toward her a single red rose.

"Oh, Antonio," she murmured, her heart light with happiness as she took the perfectly shaped flower.

"It's a sign of passion and beauty, which describes how I feel about you, Rissa. A way to say, 'I love you'—and, to coin my grandfather's phrase, my way of saying that 'you'll always be the rose of my life.' And this," he said, bringing his other hand from behind him, which she now saw held a snowy white rose, "refers to innocence and purity. Also reassurance 'that the giver is worthy of your love.' But when you put a white rose and a red rose together—"

"It means unity," Marissa finished for him, feeling happy tears prick her eyes and her voice as she carefully took the second flower and held it with the red one.

"Not bad for a crash course in floriography?" He grinned.

"Not bad at all. Oh, Antonio, I do love you! God was so good to give you to me for a husband." She again looped her arms around his neck, the flowers dangling from one hand, and kissed him without reserve. After a long, delicious moment, she pulled away.

"Let's eat in," she whispered. "I'd rather not share you with anyone tonight."

"Funny—I was just going to suggest the same thing." His murmured words were coupled with a smile that melted her into a warm pool of joy, and his eyes were twinkling. "And for the same reason," he added roguishly, a twinkle in his eye.

To Marissa's squeal of shocked delight, he swung her up from the ocean-blue carpet into the desired harbor of his strong arms.

A Letter To Our Readers

Dear Reader:

In order that we might better contribute to your reading enjoyment, we would appreciate your taking a few minutes to respond to the following questions. We welcome your comments and read each form and letter we receive. When completed, please return to the following:

Fiction Editor
Heartsong Presents
PO Box 719
Uhrichsville, Ohio 44683

1. Did you enjoy reading *A Single Rose* by Pamela Griffin?
   ❑ Very much! I would like to see more books by this author!
   ❑ Moderately. I would have enjoyed it more if

   _____

   _____

   _____

2. Are you a member of **Heartsong Presents**? ❑ Yes ❑ No
   If no, where did you purchase this book? _____

   _____

3. How would you rate, on a scale from 1 (poor) to 5 (superior), the cover design? _____

4. On a scale from 1 (poor) to 10 (superior), please rate the following elements.

   ____ Heroine   ____ Plot
   ____ Hero   ____ Inspirational theme
   ____ Setting   ____ Secondary characters

5. These characters were special because?_____
_____
_____

6. How has this book inspired your life?_____
_____
_____

7. What settings would you like to see covered in future
   Heartsong Presents books? _____
   _____
   _____

8. What are some inspirational themes you would like to see
   treated in future books? _____
   _____
   _____

9. Would you be interested in reading other **Heartsong
   Presents** titles? ❏ Yes ❏ No

10. Please check your age range:
    ❏ Under 18   ❏ 18-24
    ❏ 25-34   ❏ 35-45
    ❏ 46-55   ❏ Over 55

Name_____
Occupation _____
Address _____
City_____ State_____ Zip_____

Heart♥ong

CONTEMPORARY ROMANCE IS CHEAPER BY THE DOZEN!

Any 12
Heartsong
Presents titles
for only
$28.00*

Buy any assortment of twelve *Heartsong Presents* **titles and save 25% off of the already discounted price of $2.97 each!**

*plus $2.00 shipping and handling per order and sales tax where applicable.

HEARTSONG PRESENTS TITLES AVAILABLE NOW:

(If ordering from this page, please remember to include it with the order form.)

Presents

Great Inspirational Romance at a Great Price!

Heartsong Presents books are inspirational romances in contemporary and historical settings, designed to give you an enjoyable, spirit-lifting reading experience. You can choose wonderfully written titles from some of today's best authors like Hannah Alexander, Andrea Boeshaar, Yvonne Lehman, Tracie Peterson, and many others.

When ordering quantities less than twelve, above titles are $2.97 each.
Not all titles may be available at time of order.

HEARTSONG ♥ PRESENTS

Love Stories
Are Rated G!

That's for godly, gratifying, and of course, great! If you love a thrilling love story but don't appreciate the sordidness of some popular paperback romances, **Heartsong Presents** is for you. In fact, **Heartsong Presents** is the premiere inspirational romance book club featuring love stories where Christian faith is the primary ingredient in a marriage relationship.

Sign up today to receive your first set of four, never-before-published Christian romances. Send no money now; you will receive a bill with the first shipment. You may cancel at any time without obligation, and if you aren't completely satisfied with any selection, you may return the books for an immediate refund!

Imagine. . .four new romances every four weeks—two historical, two contemporary—with men and women like you who long to meet the one God has chosen as the love of their lives. . .all for the low price of $10.99 postpaid.

To join, simply complete the coupon below and mail to the address provided. **Heartsong Presents** romances are rated G for another reason: They'll arrive Godspeed!

YES! Sign me up for Heartsng!

NEW MEMBERSHIPS WILL BE SHIPPED IMMEDIATELY!
Send no money now. We'll bill you only $10.99 post-paid with your first shipment of four books. Or for faster action, call toll free 1-800-847-8270.

NAME _____

ADDRESS _____

CITY _____ STATE _____ ZIP _____

MAIL TO: HEARTSONG PRESENTS, P.O. Box 721, Uhrichsville, Ohio 44683
or visit www.heartsongpresents.com